Praise for the Ren

"The Lavene duet can always be counted on for an enjoyable whodunit." — *Midwest Book Review*

"This jolly series...serves up medieval murder and mayhem." — *Publishers Weekly*

"[A] terrific mystery series." — MyShelf.com

"The Renaissance Faire Mysteries are always an enjoyable read . . . Joyce and Jim Lavene provide a complex exciting murder mystery that amateur sleuth fans will appreciate."
— *Midwest Book Review*

BEWITCHING BOOTS

This story starts out after Jessie and Chase's wedding and already rumors are spreading that they are breaking up. Chase is training new knights and Jessie is wrapped up with the museum but as soon as they find time they are going to nip those rumors in the bud. When Princess Isabelle is found dead catching the killer becomes their #1 priority. Detective Almond is trying to catch a killer with Chase's assistance but Jessie is doing her own investigation.

All our favorite characters are back including Wanda, the blue ghost, and they are joined by some great new characters too! It is that time of year when new people are auditioning to became actors or acts at the faire and there are some very unusual "creatures" roaming the cobblestones.
~ Lori Caswell
continued . . .

MURDEROUS MATRIMONY

This story has a great mystery with plenty of suspects to keep us guessing – Fabulous characters including a ghost – Takes place in a fantastic setting. I love reading stories that leave me smiling at the end with a few giggles throughout and anxious for the next book.

~ Lori Caswell

PERILOUS PRANKS

This novella whets your appetite for the next book in the Renaissance Faire Mystery series - Murderous Matrimony, coming in November 2013. This is a quick fun read. It will keep you turning the pages so you can find out whodunit. The story is well plotted and will keep you intrigued with quirky characters and red herrings galore. Well, Joyce and Jim have done it again they never disappoint. So if you like your mystery with the fun of a Renaissance Faire, then you should be reading Perilous Pranks. — **Cheryl Green**

TREACHEROUS TOYS

The latest Renaissance Faire Mystery (see Harrowing Hats, Deadly Daggers and Ghastly Glass) is an engaging whodunit made fresh by changing the season as the heroine provides a tour of the Renaissance Faire Village during Christmas (instead of the summer). This exciting amateur sleuth (with Jesse's success rate on solving homicides while risking her life on cases the cops fumble; she should turn pro to pay her bills) is filled with quirky characters as team Lavene provide another engaging murder investigation. ~ Harriet Klausner

continued . . .

HARROWING HATS

"The reader will have a grand time. This is an entertaining read with a well-crafted plot. Readers of the series will not be disappointed. New readers will want to glom the backlist so they don't miss a single minute." —*Fresh Fiction*

DEADLY DAGGERS

"The Lavene duet can always be counted on for an enjoyable whodunit . . . Filled with twists and red herrings, *Deadly Daggers* is a delightful mystery." — *Midwest Book Review*

"Will keep you entertained from the first duel to the last surprise . . . If you like fun reads that will let you leave this world for a time, this series is for you." —*The Romance Readers Connection*

"Never a dull moment! Filled with interesting characters, a fast-paced story, and plenty of humor, this series never lets its readers down . . . You're bound to feel an overwhelming craving for a giant turkey leg and the urge to toast to the king's health with a big mug of ale as you enjoy this thematic cozy mystery!" —*Fresh Fiction*

GHASTLY GLASS

"A unique look at a renaissance faire. This is a colorful, exciting amateur sleuth mystery filled with quirky characters who endear themselves to the reader as Joyce and Jim Lavene write a delightful whodunit." — *Midwest Book Review*

continued . . .

WICKED WEAVES

"This jolly series debut . . . serves up medieval murder and mayhem." — *Publishers Weekly*

"A new, exciting . . . series . . . Part of the fun of this solid whodunit is the vivid description of the Renaissance Village; anyone who has not been to one will want to go . . . Cleverly developed." — *Midwest Book Review*

Fatal Fairies

By

Joyce and Jim Lavene

Chapter One

"I wish Chase wasn't Village Bailiff."

The cries of 'Hear Ye, Hear Ye' were still echoing in my ears. The town crier was making sure everyone knew that a fairy named Apple Blossom had been found dead in the Good Luck Fountain on the Village Green.

It was nearly the one-year anniversary of our wedding—Chase and me. We had plans for the occasion which would now be tossed out the window so he could spend every waking moment looking for Apple Blossom's killer.

Don't get me wrong—I'm curious about these things too. I want to help. I love to work with him to figure it out.

But on our wedding anniversary? Seriously?

"Terrible news about the fairy, wasn't it?" Manawydan Argall was my assistant at the Art and Craft Museum. I called him Manny because it was too hot for such a big name. "I hope Chase can find the killer quickly."

"If they wouldn't have been here, it wouldn't have

happened."

This was the first 'official' Fairy Week at *Renaissance Faire Village and Marketplace*—my home.

There were thousands of fairies from the East Coast Fairy Guild. We had hundreds of flirty fairies that lived and visited here every day, wearing barely their underwear and wings.

Thousands of them were way too many. But the Village liked large numbers and they made those decisions, not me.

It might have been selfish, but as I stood in the hot August sun that day wearing twenty pounds of clothing while fairies pranced by with their little crowns and magic wands, I wished that Chase wasn't going to have to look for Apple Blossom's killer.

If that was evil, so be it. I was ready for the consequences.

"That's harsh, even for you," Manny said. "And it's bad press for the Village."

"I know." I adjusted a few pairs of delicate fairy wings that were hanging in the museum this week. I really felt bad about hating the fairies and about Apple Blossom dying in the fountain.

"I'm sorry." Manny kept his black hair neatly trimmed and wore large glasses. He was short, barely five feet, and always wore dapper Victorian suits with vests, rather than the normal Renaissance garb.

He was recently out of college with a degree in the Arts. His parents were the king and queen of a small but wealthy African nation. He was my right hand man at the museum, knowing what I wanted almost before I did. I'd come to depend on him, and he'd never let me down.

"It's okay." I sighed. "Going to Europe for a week with Chase probably wasn't a good idea anyway. And what's a first wedding anniversary? I don't think it even has a theme—gold, silver, ruby, crystal. It's not a big deal."

To make matters worse, I was worried about Chase too. He'd been helping his brother and father out of a jam. I guess it wasn't enough that his father had to go to prison for insider trading.

Now his father and his brother, Morgan Stanley Manhattan, had created some kind of Ponzi scheme back in Arizona. It had gone sour, and they'd turned to Chase for help. He'd flown out there several times and spent all his time on the laptop trying to dig them out of the hole they were in.

The result? Chase was grumpy and unhappy most of the time. I tried to stay out of it. I had my own problems with my brother, Tony. He wanted to get married again. How could I tell Chase not to help his family when I had to be there for mine?

"Actually, it does have a significator. It's paper." Manny grinned, his perfect teeth very white in his dark face. "Maybe you'll still have a few days to go away for your anniversary. We should help him."

I sank down on one of the benches along the museum wall as a dozen crying fairies came in out of the sun. They were mourning their dead friend who seemed to have been murdered in broad daylight with thousands of people standing around but no one had even noticed until a few hours later.

She'd been found face up in the fountain. Chase said she'd been strangled. Someone had been incredibly daring to have done such a thing.

"You know, I just don't have it in me to help him investigate this time, Manny."

"Is it because she's a fairy and you don't like fairies?"

"No. Not just that. It's a little of everything." Naturally I couldn't tell him about Chase's father and brother being stupid, greedy pigs who might still go to prison. Or my fears that they might take Chase with them. "I think I'll sit this one out."

He stared at me and finally put his hand on my forehead. "You must be ill. For Jessie Morton-Manhattan to ignore a murder in the Village there is something very wrong."

"You could say that." I lowered my voice. "But not too loudly, please."

Looking around at my carefully crafted museum decor made my head hurt. Where I would normally have had Renaissance art and craftsmen creating beautiful works of wood, stone, or fabric for my visitors, I now had plastic fairy crowns, polyester wings, and other fairy paraphernalia.

King Harold and Queen Olivia of Ren Faire Village—along with a handful of marketing gurus—had decided a few months ago that I should stock tons of cheap fairy ware in the museum. That way if any of the fairies didn't come properly equipped with wands or wings, they could buy them from me.

It was a terrible idea. It had made the museum a big gift shop. But I got a pat on the head and was told to do my part for the Village. I knew it wasn't really my museum, though I liked to think of it that way. I was the director, employed by the Village and the parent company, theme park giant, Adventure Land.

But I had a plan which might still save me from what felt like a tidal wave.

My ace in the hole came through the door. Canyon Britt was the answer to my prayers. He was big—six-foot-four, large, muscular chest, and shoulders made for armor. He was good on a horse and had jousted several times during his college career at the Village. Canyon was also charismatic and handsome. His blond hair was bleached by the hot South Carolina sun, and his blue eyes twinkled. He was every inch the epitome of a surfer dude turned knight.

"Lady Jessie." He bowed elegantly, his red cloak sliding over one shoulder. "I have been searching for the Bailiff. Have you seen him? I am keeping the crime scene open for him. I'm sure he'll want to take a look."

"Don't worry about him," I told Canyon. "I'm sure Detective Almond is here already. You're Chase's assistant. Take charge of the investigation for the Village."

He bowed again. "My lady? I am not the Bailiff."

"Just pretend you are," I told him. "You work with the Bailiff. Chase can't be everywhere. Find out what you can and report back to him later."

"Of course, Lady Jessie. I swear it will be done!" Manny's dark eyes were unhappy after Canyon left. "Chase isn't going to like this."

He didn't realize that I'd convinced the new personnel director to hire a second-in-command for Chase.

My brilliant scheme included having Canyon take over as Village Bailiff or law keeper while we were on our European second honeymoon as well as helping him the rest of the year. I hadn't even known about Apple Blossom's death at the time, but it made sense to me.

Being Village Bailiff was a more than a one-man, full-time position. Chase needed someone to take his place occasionally when he was on the other side of the Village and someone jumped in the fountain and refused to get out. Or a camel got loose. Or there was a visitor problem at one of the eating establishments. Or someone was stuck at the top of the climbing wall.

There were hundreds of incidents every day. Add that up to the Village being open seven days a week, every day except Christmas and Thanksgiving, and you get the picture.

There wasn't always a murder investigation. Renaissance Faire Village was mostly a quiet, peaceful place. But when something big happened, it added to Chase's normal responsibilities and became completely insane.

"Really?" Manny questioned. "You think Chase will want Canyon to take over a murder investigation? I find that doubtful."

"That's his job. He's supposed to do things the Bailiff would normally do," I explained. "There's no point in him being here if he doesn't decrease Chase's workload."

He patted me on the shoulder. "You know, Jessie, you don't look like you've been sleeping well. Maybe you should go home and grab a nap. I'll keep an eye on the museum. I'm sure you'll be ready to solve Apple Blossom's murder when you get up."

"Thanks." I got to my feet, towering over him at my height of six feet. "I'm going to take you up on that. I might even grab some ginger cookies and tea from Mrs. Potts's shop. That's how convinced I am that this is all going to work out."

I walked down the cobblestones to the Dungeon where Chase and I lived. We had the upstairs apartment. The fake jail cells were on the ground floor where the plastic prisoners were kept. They cried and begged for mercy when the front door opened—courtesy of the special effects.

It could be very unnerving to get up during the night and hear them.

Of course everyone was talking about the dead fairy. Phil Ferguson from the *Sword Spotte* was standing with Fred the Red Dragon, lamenting that someone had died in the Village.

Phil was the only sword-maker that Chase would buy his swords from. I preferred Daisy Reynolds at *Swords and Such*. Both of their work was fine, but I liked Daisy better.

"I hope Chase can find the killer," Fred said from inside his red dragon costume. "It makes me nervous when someone dies here."

"I agree." Little Bo Peep tried to pass us, desperate to keep up with her sheep. "I was just near the fountain and didn't see Chase anywhere. Who is that new man, Jessie? Is he taking Chase's place?"

"Is someone taking the Bailiff's job?" Paul Samuels rubbed his hand over his balding head before replacing his green cap. He was the owner of the bookstore, *Rare Reads*, and had also started a Village newspaper. "I should be privy to this information, if so."

Fred nudged Phil with his elbow. "He said he should be a privy."

Phil rubbed his belly where the big dragon elbow had bumped him. "Go read a book, Fred. There's more than one kind of privy."

"Chase doesn't have to take care of everything in the Village," I said. "Why don't you try herding the elephants, breaking up fights at the *Monastery Bakery*, and then solving murders on the side? He's only human, you know."

They all stepped back to let me go by. I figured they knew not to mess with me about this. Everyone knew how I felt about Chase—and fairies.

I hurried past the other shops on my way home. On the *Dutchman's Stage* several loud singers were performing humorous skits. I got by the *Pleasant Pheasant* without anyone else bothering me and ignored the swaggering pirates on their way back to the *Queen's Revenge*. Their ship was anchored in Mirror Lake near the castle.

King Harold had sent a page to fetch Chase. The teenager was waiting at the door. I re-directed him to find Canyon at the Good Luck Fountain where the fairy had died. The young man thanked me graciously with a bow and the removal of his huge feathered hat.

There were several visitors in the Dungeon looking at the tortured plastic figures. I ignored them and went quickly up the stairs to our apartment, locking the door behind me and taking a deep breath.

So far, so good. Now I just had to wait for Chase's reaction to what I had set in motion.

* * *

I woke up after a pleasant dream where Chase and I were swimming naked in warm, blue water off the coast of Greece.

Not wanting to leave that wonderful place quickly, I closed my eyes and drifted in and out. This was definitely better than dealing with a fairy convention and a murder in the Village.

"Hey, beautiful," a voice whispered near my ear. "Just stay right here. I've got some free time."

I smiled as I rolled over from the middle of the bed. Already my strategy to help my wonderful husband was working. He was so relaxed that he didn't even sound like himself.

He climbed into bed beside me. "I wasn't expecting you for lunch today."

I put my arms around him. Something wasn't right. Chase was bigger—bulkier.

My bed partner licked my ear.

I opened my eyes and gasped. "You're not Chase!"

Canyon grinned. "Thank goodness. I wouldn't have you here if I was."

It only took a moment to grab the blanket and get out of bed. As soon as I was on my feet with my eyes wide open, I knew something was very, very wrong.

Chapter Two

"What are you doing here? Where's Chase?"

Canyon rolled over and smiled lazily at me. "I'm here because this is the Dungeon where the Village Bailiff lives. You're here because you're my wonderful, sexy lady. Are you talking about Chase Manhattan, that glory-seeking jouster? Maybe he's with the queen. You never know with him."

"What?" It was the only intelligible word I could get out of my mouth. "Chase is the Village Bailiff. He has been since Roger Trent retired."

It was a joke—a prank. We all loved pranks at the Village. I'd done many of them myself. Some of them were quite good. This one wasn't.

"Okay. I get it. It's a prank, right?" I laughed. "This is a big, stupid prank. Now get out of my bed and find Chase."

"Quit talking about Manhattan, Jessie, and get back in

bed. I've only got a few minutes before that stupid Detective Almond gets to the Village to investigate the fairy murder." He smiled and put his hands above his head. "Plenty of time for the good stuff, my fine lady."

I started to say 'what' again and stopped myself. I couldn't keep repeating that word. It wasn't doing any good. None of this made any sense, except for the prank angle. I stuck to my first impression.

"Canyon, Chase will kick your butt if he finds you here. I know you think you're tough, but Chase has a lot of experience dealing with bad pranks and employees who forget who they are."

He finally sat up and stared hard at me. "Is something wrong with you? I heard you left your apprenticeship at *Rare Reads* early today. You look pale. You're not sick, are you?"

I watched him as he ran into the bathroom to gargle and spray himself with Lysol. Canyon was terrified of getting sick. I'd kept that fact to myself when I advised the new director to hire him. How often would it come up when he was policing the Village?

That's when I really looked around myself. This was totally a prank. It had to be, and yet the best prank in the world couldn't make the Dungeon apartment look as it had before Chase and I were married.

A wandering sorcerer had magically made the apartment larger on the inside. It still looked exactly the same on the outside. It was difficult to explain. You had to see it.

When I'd moved in with Chase, years before we were married, the apartment had consisted of a single room that was a bedroom, tiny kitchen, and bathroom all rolled into one. It was all the two of us could do not to bump into one another as we walked around it.

When I'd come home from the museum that day, I'd come home to the large version of the apartment. Now it had gone back to being the small one again. I'd accomplished some pretty awesome pranks in my day, but this wasn't possible. No prank could make this happen—unless it was a magic prank.

Magic had come to Renaissance Faire Village last year at about the same time that Chase and I got married. It had changed everything for those of us who lived here as well as for those who visited. No one could ever be certain what they would see or experience. It had started with a ghost but had escalated to a witch and a sorcerer—and maybe a man who made magic shoes.

Could this prank be the work of one of the magic users that now called the Village their home? Or was it the sorcerer who had visited us and changed it in the first place? Maybe he'd returned.

Canyon pulled on his clothes and shoved his feet into thick sandals. He pushed his shaggy blond hair out of his eyes and kept his distance.

"You should pay a visit to the first aid station, Jessie" he suggested. "Wanda should be able to tell if you're sick."

"Wanda? Blue ghost Wanda?" I laughed, but I was beginning to panic. "I don't think there's anything she can do for me. I'm sorry. You might not be able to see her. Not everyone can."

"There's something really bad wrong with you, my beautiful lady. I'll tell *Rare Reads* that you won't be back today. You go see Wanda or go to the hospital. You might be having a breakdown or something."

He left the apartment, and I hurriedly dressed. I didn't want to be caught with my pants down again, so to speak. But even my clothes were different.

When I'd done apprenticeships around the Village to write my thesis for my doctorate, *Proliferation of Medieval Crafts in Modern Times*, I'd had to dress to suit each position. Usually long, coarse-knit skirts with pockets and blouses. Sometimes I wore britches and shirts, dressing like a man.

Canyon had said I was working as an apprentice at *Rare Reads* where they printed and bound books as well as selling new ones. My dress was rough linen covered by an ink-stained white blouse and apron. I looked at my hands. They were covered in ink. My face had ink blotches on it too.

As Director of the *Art and Craft Museum*, I dressed as I pleased—usually as a high-born lady with better quality skirts and boots. I would never have walked around the Village dressed in these clothes.

It was as though I'd gone back in time, which I sincerely hoped was impossible even with magic in the Village. What was going on?

I reassured myself again that this had to be a prank. I had to find the prankster and let him or her know that this was over. I knew what was going on. They couldn't fool me. Then life would go back to normal.

The first thing I had to do was find Chase. I knew he wouldn't be in on it. He wasn't like that. Despite Canyon's opinion of him, Chase wasn't a prankster. He was serious, diligent, and hardworking. He never appreciated my pranks and had passed on many great opportunities to accomplish his own.

Since Canyon had said Chase was working as a jouster again, I headed toward the Field of Honor. Somehow, he and I would make sense of this. Even if we didn't know exactly what was going on, we'd figure it out. It was the way it worked between us.

I ignored everyone who spoke to me on the way to the field. I needed answers more than casual companionship. Some of them could even be in on it. I kept my eyes open for Wanda —the dead, blue version of the woman. She could pull off something like this since she was a ghost. I'd seen her do some crazy things.

The Queen's Joust was just finishing up as I trudged up the hill to the outdoor arena. The bleachers were completely full with screaming fans, many of which were holding signs with Chase's name on them.

Just like the old days when he was everyone's favorite jouster.

And there he was on the field in his shiny silver armor.

His face shield was raised as he held his lance high showing his victory over his opponent, a smaller knight on a brown horse.

I smiled when I saw him, tears starting to my eyes. I lifted my skirts and ran the rest of the way to reach him, despite the heat of the day. Chase would know what to do. He'd have some answers or know where to get them. He always knew what to do.

By the time I reached him, he was leaving the *Field of Honor*. He'd received his accolades from the crowds who were still chanting his name. Queen Olivia was smiling and waving a rose at him.

Dozens of jousting groupies were standing so close to him that his horse couldn't move. Finally his squire grabbed the horse's reins to get him back to the area behind the viewing stands. Chase needed to get cleaned up and out of jousting gear so he could rest before the next contest. So did his horse.

I knew where they were going and skirted the crowd to head that way. Surely the stables and the dressing rooms for the jousters couldn't have changed that much from when I was a squire a few years before.

Chase's name was above the door to his dressing room. There was a big gold star with it that had never been there when he was a jouster. I stared at it curiously before going inside to wait for him.

It wasn't long before he came in from the heat. His squire was a tall, thin boy with badly cut hair. He began immediately helping him remove his armor. Chase unfastened his gloves and dropped them to the floor.

"Will that be all, sir?" the boy asked in an eager voice.

"That's all, Emerson. Next joust isn't until four. Get some rest and don't forget."

The boy nodded and left the dressing room. Chase sat in a chair, shirtless, as he drained a bottle of water in one gulp. He was covered in sweat, but there were no showers here. He'd have to wait until he got home.

He sounded like Chase. He looked like Chase. That gave me the courage to come out of hiding.

"Jessie?" He frowned. "What are you doing here?"

"I'm so glad to see you." I jumped in his lap and wrapped my arms around him, big sobs coming from my chest. "I was so worried something had happened to you."

He didn't put his arms around me, patting my back in a careful manner. "Does Canyon know you're here?"

"Canyon?" I wiped the tears away. "Why are you asking about him? You can't be in on this prank. You hate pranks. You wouldn't do this to me."

His wonderful brown eyes were filled with compassion. "So you and Canyon broke up?"

I stood and stamped my foot. I hadn't done that in a long time. I'd been trying to learn to control my temper.

"What's going on? Is this a sick joke, or are you trying to tell me you don't love me anymore?"

"Jessie, we've always been good friends. I don't recall ever talking about love. Are you okay?"

"This can't be happening." I paced the small floor. "I finally have everything I ever wanted, and now it's gone."

"Would you like some water? Maybe you should sit down for a few minutes. Were you out in the sun a lot today?"

"No! I don't want to sit down. I wasn't in the sun, and I'm not sick. I'm also not sleeping with Canyon. You and I have been married for almost a year. Don't you remember?"

"I think I should get Wanda for you," he volunteered. "Or I could look for Canyon if that's better."

"Quit trying to be so helpful. You're just making it worse."

I paced for another few minutes while he watched me.

Wanda. Wanda had to be the key to all this. She didn't have magic, but she was a ghost. She'd set all this up to get even with me for dyeing her blue before she was killed. I should have realized that she'd want revenge for that at some time. What she'd done, ruining our wedding, wasn't enough.

It wasn't like I'd killed her. It was just a series of unfortunate events.

"Chase. You have to believe me. Look at the wedding ring that you made for me." I held out my hand, but my ring was gone.

He took my hand and smiled at me. "Don't worry, Jessie. We'll find someone who can help you. You wait right here, okay? I'll get help."

I was too dumbfounded to speak. He kissed my sweaty forehead and left the dressing room.

There was no time to waste. I needed to marshal my forces and figure out what I should do next. I had to find Wanda and get the truth out of her before something happened and things couldn't go back the way they were before.

Looking both ways before I went out, I left the dressing room and ran along the edge of the fence that led from the *Field of Honor* back down into the Village. I thought Chase might be headed toward Wanda's first aid clinic near the castle, but instead, he'd been stopped by Merlin, the Village magician, on the other side of the blacksmith's shop. He couldn't see me. That was probably for the best.

I kept running past the Lady Fountain as King Arthur tried to pull his sword from the stone, uttering vivid, colorful oaths that impressed the visitors watching him. Mary waved to me from *Wicked Weaves*, her basket-weaving shop. Roger was talking to a customer about a large glass statue of a dragon near his shop, the *Glass Gryphon*.

Music came from the *Hawk Stage*, where Lady Lindsey was doing her twice-daily show with her pretty song birds. The Lovely Laundry Ladies were calling out to men as they passed, asking them for help with their wet bundles of clothes. I ran past *Baron's Beer and Brats* and *Polo's Pasta*.

I was pretty much out of breath by the time I reached the first aid station. I had to stand outside panting. It gave me a minute to think about what I should say and do.

Wanda was cunning, no doubt about it. She'd had to

manipulate so many things to get me to this point. She had to have help, I realized. Maybe the new witch who'd moved into the *Lady of the Lake Tavern*.

Two young men in doublets and hose were running out of the first aid station like the devil was after them. They were followed by an angry mother in a long, daffodil-yellow gown and her crying daughter.

"If that woman is a nurse," the mother said ferociously, "then I'm Madam Curie. Come on, Bella. Let's go."

I knew Wanda was in the clinic. She had that effect on everyone. I knew she'd done this to me, whatever it was. I had to make her take it all back.

I took a deep breath and went inside to face her.

Chapter Three

There she was, Wanda Le Fey, in all her living glory.

I realized there was no way she could pull off being alive again. She wasn't blue from head to toe either. Even if this was the greatest prank ever, it couldn't happen.

"Jessie." Her red lips turned up in a snarky smile. "How lovely to see you."

Wanda was the only actual Brit in the Village. No matter how hard the rest of us might try to imitate her accent, we were never quite as good. Or as subtly evil.

I was never sure how she'd managed to become a nurse, but everyone she'd ever treated had suffered for it. She always wound bandages too tightly on sprained ankles and never gave out the right medicine. I knew we should all just be thankful she wasn't a surgeon. She'd certainly have managed to cut off a limb if that were the case.

She hummed to herself as she adjusted her pink bustier

and sorted through some items on a tray.

Seeing her there in the flesh was nearly more than I could handle. Her bright red hair curled around her face, and her shrewd eyes searched for any weakness on my sure-to-be pink face. I still believed that she was at the heart of whatever was happening to me. But this was more than I'd expected. I had to sit down for a moment.

"What can we do for you today, Jessie?" she asked in a sweet voice that probably fooled some people into believing she was actually a good person.

"You can tell me what deal you made with the devil to ruin my life." I tried not to cry—she'd just take advantage of me.

"A fascinating idea, but I've had my mind on other things. Getting revenge on you can't be all I do, despite how interesting that sounds."

"How did you manage it? Did you hook up with the sorcerer again or something? He brought you back to life and then you decided to get even once and for all."

"You really are ill, poor dear. Let me take your temperature. I have a nice rectal thermometer right over here. Lie down and lift your skirt for me. There's a sweet angel."

"Forget it." I stood and fiercely faced her. "I know you've done something magical to me. Just admit it."

"I truly would love to tell you that I've done something naughty to you, Jessie." She smiled as she toyed with the thermometer. "But honestly, ducks, I've been too busy. Come back later. Maybe I'll think of something fun by then."

"I'm not leaving until you tell me how to get Chase back."

She laughed. "So that's it. You and Canyon are finally over, and you're on the hunt for someone new. Well, don't look at me when it comes to Chase Manhattan. That's a one 'knight' stand I never had in the Village. Not for lack of trying, mind you. I'd certainly be happy to let him dip his toe in my pool anytime."

Had the entire Village gone insane? Why did everyone

think I was sleeping with Canyon? Why couldn't anyone remember that Chase and I were married?

I picked up the only thing I could imagine using as a weapon—a magazine—rolled it and held it toward her in a threatening manner. I was bigger and taller than her. Even without a sword I could beat the snot out of her.

"Easy, easy." Chase came up behind me and grabbed the magazine. "Wanda, something is really wrong with Jessie. Can you help her?"

"Of course, my love." She smiled in a possessive manner. "Just heave her up here on the old exam table, and we'll see what the problem is."

He lifted me easily in his arms. His long brown braid came around on his shoulder, and I held it to my face as I started crying.

"Please don't let her hurt me," I pleaded with him. "I've really had a bad day."

"*Shh.*" He sat on the exam table with me on his lap.

He was six-foot-eight, two hundred and fifty pounds of muscle covered in dark leather, and wearing a gold earring. He was the most understanding and wonderful man I'd ever known. I loved him with all my heart. This had to be something we could fix. Chase and I were meant to be together.

"Wanda will make it better. Right, Wanda?" He smiled at her.

He'd always trusted her. I could never figure out why.

"That's right." Wanda put her soft hand on my forehead. "She is rather heated, isn't she? Probably sunstroke or heat apathy. I'll just call an ambulance, shall I? I'm sure she needs a hospital."

"No!" I surprised Chase when I jumped up "No hospital. No Wanda-care. I'll see you later after I've figured this out. I love you, Chase. Please don't forget that."

"Jessie . . . wait."

Chase was fast, but I was faster. I ran through all the paths and byways I knew from the first aid station to the

Main Gate. I suddenly knew exactly what I had to do.

I had to visit one of our newest residents, Madame Lucinda. She knew everything about magic and strange things that had happened in the Village. She'd know what Wanda had done. She'd know how to set it right.

I got past the minstrels at the gate as they played their lutes and harps for visitors. Flower girls tossed their petals at the ladies and gentlemen. Dancers and joke-telling jugglers were there too, wishing everyone a good evening as they departed.

And finally I ran through a group of Robin Hood's Merry Men to reach the purple and gold tent where Madame Lucinda lived and told fortunes for her visitors.

But the tent was gone, as it had been before the coming of magic to the Village. All that was there was an old wood sign that said, "Village fun this way" and an arrow pointing toward the cobblestones.

I looked across the street at the three brick manor houses that had never been used until I'd opened the Art and Craft Museum last year. The wonderful houses were empty again, their silent faces elegantly turned to welcome visitors coming through the Main Gate.

"Jessie!" It was Robin Hood in his forest green doublet and tights. "Where are you headed? You look upset. I heard you lost your apprenticeship at the bookstore today."

"I lost everything else." I was on the verge of hysteria. "But I didn't lose an apprenticeship."

Toby Gates had played Robin Hood at the Village for as long as I could remember. He was a nice guy who loved his role and loved living in the five acres of woods that were known as Sherwood Forest. Every year, he picked up a few more Merry Men and Women. They lived in the large tree houses together and spent their time stealing toaster ovens from residents while amusing visitors.

We sat on the steps of one of the manor houses. I was confused and ready to give up. Maybe I'd gone crazy. Maybe this was my life and I just couldn't remember. I tried to hold on to what I thought my life should be, but it kept slipping through my hands.

"It's getting late." He nodded at the Main Gate where large groups of people were noisily filing out to the parking lot. "You're welcome to spend the night in the forest if you don't have anywhere to go."

His face told me that he'd heard about my 'breakup' with Canyon. Naturally he assumed that breakup also put me out on the cobblestones.

But I wasn't that woman anymore.

I squared my shoulders, held my chin high, and smiled at him.

"I'm fine. Thank you. I'm not sure what's wrong right now. But I'll figure it out."

He took my hand. "Just remember you're always welcome in the forest. Let me know if you need anything."

His words were so sweet that I hugged him until I saw his present Lady Marion coming our way, kicking her little booted feet on the cobblestones as she walked. She wouldn't have been so upset if she'd known how many Lady Marions there had been in the forest, including me for a time.

"Thank you. I think you need to go now unless you want to find a lady-sized dagger in your back tonight."

Robin laughed his signature laugh with his hands on his hips and head thrown back. "You know I love the ladies, and they love me."

"I know."

"But a friend like you is a friend forever, Jessie, my dear." He bowed and kissed my hand. "Now I must away to stave off yon lady's harsh words."

I curtsied to him, holding the sides of my ink-stained gown. "A good night to you, sir."

The visitors leaving the village paused to take a few pictures and exclaim over our fascinating conversation. Robin and I posed together for them, and then he made his escape into the forest with his men and Lady Marion.

I watched the visitors leaving with a mournful eye,

wishing I could walk through the gate too. But there was no one out there for me. My life was here with Chase, and even my brother, Tony. Our only living relative had died many years before.

What was I supposed to do?

Everything was familiar, and yet completely changed. Chase wasn't the Village Bailiff any longer. I wasn't the museum director. And yet, *Rare Reads* was in the Village. It had only been here since last year. How could some things have stayed the same and others changed?

As I struggled to understand, I saw Chase coming toward me. I loved everything about him, from his kindness to his intelligence, and the wonderful way he dealt with people. I could see by the look on his handsome face that he was about to find an answer for me too.

How could Canyon ever have taken his place as Bailiff?

"Jessie." Chase smiled and held out his hands as though I was a skittish mare. "I know you're in some kind of trouble. I figured you could use a friendly face and a place to spend the night."

I got to my feet, excited that I'd made some kind of breakthrough with him. Maybe he was starting to remember who I was and why I was in his life.

"Thank you." I might not have been interested in spending the night in the woods with Robin Hood, but I'd jump at the chance to spend the night with Chase. "You don't know what this means to me."

"Sorry I'm late." My brother, Tony, came up behind me. "Chase said you've been having a nervous breakdown or something. I'm here for you, Jessie. My place isn't very big, but I'm sure we can squeeze in together for a while."

I was so stunned that Chase had brought Tony to help me—my crazy brother of all people. Chase knew what a handful he could be. How many times had we bailed him out of trouble?

"Really?" My gaze stayed on Chase's. "This is it? I spend the night with Tony? That's the answer?"

Chase's expression was apologetic. "I'm living with Princess Isabelle at the castle, or I'd ask you to stay with me. Sorry, Jessie. Better Tony than Canyon, if the two of you are breaking up. I could check with Village housing tomorrow to see if anything is available."

"No. That's okay. I can figure this out. I can check on Village housing myself, if I need to. Thanks Chase."

He put his hand on mine. "I'm sorry you're going through a bad time. Let me know if I can do anything else."

"Sure." I managed to smile at him even though tears were welling in my eyes. At least he probably thought it was because I was breaking up with Canyon.

To make matters worse, one of the pop-up, late evening thunderstorms that frequently hit the Village from the Atlantic chose that moment to rear its ugly head. Bursts of thunder and lightning came first, followed by drenching rain that swept the cobblestones and sent what visitors were left quickly out the gate.

Tony and I scrambled too. The last look I had at Chase, he was standing in the rain, watching me leave. Was that a trace of sadness in his eyes?

I couldn't tell because there was too much rain in mine. And really, I hoped he was miserable without me.

We went to one of the Village housing sheds. It was more like a shack than a house. Several people were living together in three bedrooms, a kitchen, and a bathroom. There was no air-conditioning, and it had a lingering scent of dirty socks. It reminded me of being in college.

Most of the workers who were housed in these places were college and high school students. There were also some full-time, adult employees. I stepped over dirty clothes and avoided discarded bits of armor, wigs, and staffs. There was also a horse's head and the front half of a cow.

"Mi casa—you know what I mean." Tony sat on one of the lumpy old chairs. "You can stay here as long as you need to. No one will notice another person."

"Thanks." I glanced around the dirty room. I'd lived in

places like this over summer break for years while I was in college. I'd finally found my own small space but had given it up to live with Chase.

"What happened to you?" he asked. "You're usually too well organized for something like this. I guess you didn't see it coming with Canyon, huh?"

I put my hand to my head. It might be the only opportunity I had to tell anyone what really happened. I knew Tony wouldn't believe me—might even laugh at me. I didn't care. It was a release just to say it out loud.

He stared at me with our father's brown eyes. He was left handed like him too. We were both six feet tall, but it looked better on him. His brown hair had a bit of curl in it from our mother's side. Mine was stick-straight.

"Hey. That's pretty cool," he said when I'd finished explaining. "So you're a time traveler. How'd you do it?"

That was one question I wasn't expecting.

"I don't think this is time traveling. Some of the shops and people in the Village are from ten years ago, but some of them are new. Even worse, some of the people are dead."

Tony sat up straight. "Like who? Am I dead in the future? Is Chase dead? What about that hot girl that sells pretzels down by the *Field of Honor*?"

"You're not dead," I assured him as a few other people wandered into the conversation. They wanted to know if they were dead in the future and if I could help them time travel. Before I knew it, the entire room was filled with young men who wanted to know if I'd used a time machine and where I'd stored it.

It was a long evening full of flat beer and leftover pizza with the rain beating down on the roof. I really hadn't meant to spark a conversation about whether or not time travel was possible, or if it was happening in the Village. After one in the morning, I just kind of fell asleep in the hard chair. The voices around me kept going until much later.

But I woke abruptly when my cell phone chimed at five a.m. I'd never set an alarm on it. If I had, it certainly wouldn't have been for that time of the morning. The Village didn't open until ten. Nights were late here. No one got up before nine.

It took me a few minutes to turn off the alarm. By that time, I was completely awake. The living room was empty, but I could hear snoring from the bedrooms around me.

"Good morning, dear. I hope you're feeling better this morning."

I glanced around and finally found a short, older woman sitting in the chair beside me. She was smiling at me and kicking her little feet about a foot off the floor. She was dressed in a bright blue version of Little Red Riding Hood's hood, cape, and gown.

"I guess I'm okay," I answered carefully. "Who are you?"

She giggled, kicking her feet until her layers of blue petticoats were bouncing. "I'm Starshine, your fairy godmother, of course."

Chapter Four

"Of course." I got out of the chair and stretched. My back hurt and my legs were numb. "I'm going to get breakfast now, if I can find anything besides cold pizza to eat. I'll see you later."

"I'd rather go with you, if you don't mind. We have a lot to talk about and very little time to act on the problems that have been created by your wish."

"My wish?" I just thought yesterday was weird. "I don't remember making a wish."

"Silly girl. I wouldn't be here if you hadn't made a wish." Starshine tapped my cheek with her finger. "I suppose I would technically still be in Renaissance Faire Village if you hadn't made that wish, but I certainly wouldn't be in this hovel. I don't think you would be either."

Her voice was beautiful. It had a chiming quality to it that made it sound as though she were singing. Her hair was long and silver. It hung down her back past her waist. She was only about three feet tall, and that might only have been if she was stretching.

"Okay. I'm in. Why not?" I stared at her as I ran my fingers through my hair so it wasn't sticking up all over my head. "What wish did I make?"

She cleared her throat. *"I wish that Chase wasn't the Village Bailiff."*

I sat down again. "How did you know I said that?"

"Because I'm your fairy godmother. I hear all your wishes, Jessie, even the ones I think might be better off left unwished—such as this one. There are catastrophic side effects to this kind of wish that most people just don't realize."

"I'm asleep, right? Maybe I'm in a coma or something which would explain everything that happened yesterday and you too, with your tiny little feet. No one can walk on feet that small."

She had feet that would have been too small for some large dolls. And she kept kicking them.

"Or you made an unwise wish and you're dealing with the aftermath." She smoothed back her fine hair with a tiny hand.

For just a moment, I was terrified. Was this real? Was she right? Had I lost my mind?

Then I realized that no one really had a fairy godmother. No one is out there granting crazy wishes for unsuspecting museum directors. It was all part of the prank—a prolonged, carefully planned and executed prank to be sure. But still a prank.

"Okay. Thanks for the information. I have to go." No one was fooling me with this, and someone was going to pay when I pranked them later.

"No. Wait. You can't go out looking that way," she said.

"Are you gonna change this to a poofy, sparkly gown so I can go to the ball?"

"Some people are so hard to learn," she told me. "I gave

you exactly what you asked for. What more do you want?"

"If you really did this to me, did you think I'd be grateful?" I demanded. "Chase isn't Bailiff anymore—Canyon is. Chase is with Princess Isabelle, and I'm alone. I'm not the museum director, I'm back doing apprenticeships. None of this is a wish come true."

She smiled very kindly as though she were dealing with a slow child. "Except for the part about Chase not being Bailiff anymore. That wish has been granted. It's not my fault that you don't like the repercussions. That happens sometimes when people haven't thought through their wish. But you can change that."

"Change my life back to being happy again?" I mocked her.

"That's right. But just as you have side effects from your original wish, there could be side effects from you making changes to it."

I didn't know if I should scream or sit down and have her tell me what I should do. My life had taken a turn for the weird. Maybe it was the fault of a bad wish. Everything that had changed seemed to have something to do with me or Chase. If I could put everything right again, maybe it would change back.

"Let's say I believe you." I started pacing the miniscule uncluttered area of the room. "What would I have to do to change things?"

"Well, you'd certainly want to make Chase fall in love with you again. When you took the part of him away that wanted to be Bailiff, you lost the part of him that wanted to be with you. Human beings are very complicated that way. It's difficult to change one tiny part of them without changing other aspects."

"Okay. I took him away from Princess Isabelle once. I could probably do it again. I'd need the right circumstances, but I'm sure he still loves me. He just doesn't know it right now."

"And you'd have to solve the murder of the poor fairy

that innocently came to the Village with perfectly good intentions, only to find herself struck down in her prime."

"You mean Apple Blossom? What does that have to do with me and Chase?"

"I would've thought that was completely obvious, Jessie. Use your brain, please do. You have to get Chase to help you solve the murder. It was the basis for your wish."

"In other words if Chase doesn't get interested in being Bailiff again—"

"No happy ever after for the two of you." Her miniature, wizened face was sad as she wiped a tear from her eye.

"Wait a minute. If you knew this was going to happen when you granted my wish for him not to be Bailiff, why didn't you tell me?"

"I had no idea, my dear. Not that I could have stopped you from making your wish." Starshine straightened her shoulders. "Fairy godmothers have a certain code of ethics."

"Which doesn't include telling someone if they're going to make a wish that will ruin their lives?"

"That's right. Now, what's your plan?"

"I don't know. I need coffee and a cinnamon roll for my brain to function. Let's go."

She came along readily. The small wings on her back beat rapidly like a humming bird as she lifted up from the chair and accompanied me out the door. That really threw me. I had to be imagining all this.

Morning sunshine and the hard feel of cobblestones beneath my booted feet made me feel better. Yet, there she was beside me. Her small head bobbed back and forth like a child's checking for traffic before crossing the street. I decided to check my own sanity and ask the first person I saw if he could see her.

It was an older pirate, one of those that had been around for many years. He wore his hair braided and had a large, real, black mustache that draped across his face.

"Good morrow to you, sir," I said with a respectful head bow. "I was wondering if I might ask a boon of you."

He eyed me with the red-eyed gaze of someone who hadn't slept the night before, and reeked of rum. "Why certainly, lass. What is it ye need?"

"Here. On my right. Do you see anything?"

With one eye closed, he scanned the space beside me. "What is it yer looking for?"

"A fairy, good sir. She is little more than two feet high, dressed in a blue cape, and flying with tiny wings."

The pirate burst out laughing. "Ye obviously had an even better night than myself, lass. I only saw a green dragon on my way here! Good day to ye."

He was still laughing as he left.

"There." Starshine smiled. "Does that make you feel better, Jessie?"

"I wish it did. But when Wanda was dead, some people could see her and some couldn't. He might be one of those who couldn't."

"And did that make Wanda any less real?"

"No." I grunted. Why did all the crazy magic have to come my way? "Let's get some coffee."

I hadn't realized where Tony had brought me last night. It had been raining too hard, and I'd been too upset to notice.

We were actually close to the camel and elephant enclosure. I could smell them and hear the elephants bellowing. It was a long walk across the Village Green to reach the *Monastery Bakery*. I could have stopped at one of the spots on this side of the Village, such as *Sir Latte's Beanery*, but I preferred the coffee at the bakery. And I really needed a cinnamon roll.

The grass was wet and deep, lush green in the humid morning air. My boots were very thin and soaked right away, along with the hem of my gown. I hadn't wrangled with Portia at *Stylish Frocks* for a new costume in a long time. I wasn't looking forward to it. But sleeping in damp clothes made anything sound better.

"This is such a wonderful place," Starshine twittered as we crossed the Village. "I can understand why you'd want to live here."

We went past several performers practicing for the day. Lord Maximus had his birds of prey out, swooping down from the pale blue morning sky to get their treats. Galileo was setting up his telescope and table where he lectured on heavenly bodies—including the lovely young women who visited him.

William Shakespeare aka Pat Snyder was having an in-depth conversation with Sam Da Vinci who was a regular at the Village. The Tornado Twins, Diego and Lorenzo, were trying to make their pet pig follow Lady Godiva in her flesh-colored body suit. But the little pig was too afraid of the beautiful white horse she rode.

"It's rather like living at the circus, isn't it?" Starshine asked. "You never know where to look next."

"That's true," I agreed. "I love it. I always have. Chase does too." I frowned. "Or at least he did."

"Cheer up. Chase is still the same man you've always known and loved. You're the same person too. Life is different because of your wish, but that doesn't mean you can't be together again."

"Maybe your wishes should come with warnings."

She frowned. "You might be right. People are more complicated now than when I was a girl. There was less to get wrong when things went bad, you understand."

"When was that? When were you a girl?"

"Let me see." She screwed up her face. "I think it's been a while. I believe—no wait—I'm sure. The real Da Vinci was painting then."

"You've been alive for hundreds of years?"

"In one form or another." She stopped moving before we went through the door into the *Monastery Bakery*. "Perhaps there's something else I should tell you. I don't want it to come as too great a shock to you."

But before she could tell me, Canyon saw me and came over.

"Jessie. My lady." He made a gallant try at a graceful

bow. "Why are you telling everyone that I kicked you out? I didn't even know we'd broken up until Manhattan told me. Is something wrong between us? You know I'd do anything to make it right."

To prove himself, he put his arms around me and began kissing my neck.

Across his shoulder, I saw my fairy godmother clapping her little hands and smiling.

"Whose side are you on anyway?" I hissed. "This isn't Chase."

"No. But it is the present Bailiff who will be involved in the murder case. This is your chance to start back to where you want to be."

She was right. But she didn't have to be so happy about it.

"Are you on your way in for coffee?" Canyon asked.

"Yes. I'm so glad I ran into you." I smiled like I was happy about it too. "I wanted to talk to you about the murder in the Village. Have you started investigating that yet?"

"Not really." He held the rounded door open for me. "You know how I hate these things. I was hoping Detective Almond might solve it before I had to get involved."

Starshine flew in with us like a large, blue bird. She hovered at a table. Canyon and I took a seat.

The rough wood tables and chairs fit the Renaissance air of the bakery. This was the only place in the Village where no one paid the employees. The monks of the Brotherhood of the Sheaf took their vows to make bread seriously and did so in a religious fashion. I wasn't sure with the changes around me who was head monk at this time. I saw Brother Carl in his black robe, but Brother John was also there.

"I'll get us some coffee and cinnamon rolls," Canyon offered. "I know how you like it, honey. You just sit right here and relax."

He was trying to be nice. He just wasn't Chase.

Starshine made a buzzing sound that I hoped she wouldn't do very often. It reminded me too much of a large bee.

"Look! There he is!" she whispered.

I didn't need to look to know it was Chase. I could feel that he was close by. He and I had a bond that was difficult to explain but it was very strong. Knowing it was gone made me want to cry.

"Jessie. How are you this morning?" He sat close to me, concern in his eyes. "You look much better."

If I have to win you back, I might as well start now.

"I look like a wet dog. That's what happens when you spend the night at a frat house and sleep in wet clothes."

He laughed. "I didn't notice that part. Really. I meant you don't look so sad and confused."

"I think I've found an answer to my problem. Thanks for helping me last night. You've always been such a good friend."

It was true. For years before we were lovers, we were friends. We joked around when we saw each other. I went to watch him at Vegetable Justice where visitors and residents could hit people with squishy fruit and vegetables when they were angry at them. We liked each other before we loved each other.

We still had that between us here, wherever here was. I had to find that spark that had brought us together in a more romantic way.

"Well I'm glad things are better for you. You scared me yesterday. You know how people sometimes go off the deep end. I'm glad that didn't happen to you."

"Me too. I'll see you later."

He gave me a quick kiss on the cheek and squeezed my shoulder. It wasn't anything he wouldn't have done for any other woman in the Village that he considered a friend. That was just the way he was.

Canyon arrived with our coffee and rolls. He nodded to Chase and sat possessively beside me. "Manhattan."

Chase nodded. "Britt."

We watched Chase get into the line for coffee. Canyon

put his arm around me.

"What is it with you and him?" He stared at me. "Have you got a thing for him or something?"

"No." I sipped my coffee, feeling like a spider in the middle of a web. "Of course not."

He chuckled. "I knew it. Why would you want leftovers when you could have the main course?"

"That's what I was thinking." I smiled and touched his hand. "Now tell me what you know about the dead fairy."

Chapter Five

I convinced Canyon to walk to the Good Luck Fountain with me. I tried not to feel guilty for pretending to like being with him. This wasn't a real place anyway. I had to stay focused on what was important—getting Chase to love me and figuring out who killed the fairy.

"Don't forget he must help you solve the murder to put the universe back into its proper perspective." Starshine buzzed alongside us as we walked.

No one seemed to notice her. Chase had almost sat on top of her. Canyon couldn't see or hear her. It was like she wasn't there.

I hoped she was there. If not, I was doing all this for nothing and probably walking around in my real life like a crazy person. It made me cringe to think how worried Chase must be. Had I disappeared from our lives, and he was searching for me? Or was I there—just completely out of my mind—babbling about Canyon and fairies?

There was no way to know. I glanced at my fairy godmother and knew I had no choice but to trust her—and myself. I had to do this thing and hope for the best.

We'd reached the edge of the large, closed fountain. There was yellow police tape around it to keep out curious visitors.

"She was found here," Canyon said. "You can see the blood on the lip of the fountain. Detective Almond said she probably hit her head and fell in. He just isn't sure if it happened because someone pushed her or not."

"How is he going to decide if that's what happened?"

He shrugged. "I don't know. He does his thing and tells me when he has the answer. That's the way it works."

"Not in my Village," I muttered, walking around the fountain.

Of course the lush grass was flattened everywhere around the area. There was no way the police could find the right footprints or have any idea how many people had been here when Apple Blossom had died. Could they get fingerprints from concrete? I was pretty sure that's what the fountain was made of.

"When will you get the report from the police?" I asked.

"When they send it. What's up with you, baby?" He started to put his arms around me and then took a step back, squeezing his nose with his fingers. "You need a shower and some new clothes. Instead of worrying about this dead fairy, you better worry about yourself and your apprenticeship."

Was this what the real Canyon was like? He had always been punctual and respectful in my Village. Was this what I'd find eventually if I knew him long enough?

"Thanks for the reminder." I managed a friendly smile. "I guess I should head over to *Stylish Frocks* to see Portia about a dress. You should get on the phone with Detective Almond before the Village opens. I need to know about the fairy."

"Why? Was she a relative or something? What's this

new interest in fairies? You've always hated them."

"Don't remind me. Just get the report for me, please, Canyon?"

"Okay," he agreed reluctantly. "I'll see what I can do. Meet you for lunch today?"

"I don't know. Let's see what happens, okay? Paul might have extra work for me at the book store."

Or I might be able to find some way to have lunch with Chase.

We said goodbye, and Canyon headed toward the *Mother Goose Pavilion*. She'd lost her goose, Phineas, again. Some things were exactly the same here.

I walked up the cobblestones to *Stylish Frocks* which was near the Main Gate and the *Mermaid Lagoon*. Only the *Mermaid Lagoon* wasn't there. There was only Mirror Lake and the pirate ship *Queen's Revenge* sailing across the clear surface.

It was an awesome sight with the morning sun glinting off the water, making the white sails even brighter against the blue sky. I could hear the pirates rehearsing their skits, yelling at each other and occasionally firing a musket. They saved the cannon fire for once or twice a day or during special events. It was expensive.

They'd fired all the cannons on the day Chase and I had gotten married. Sigh.

"Don't get caught up in what hasn't happened," Starshine said as I fought to keep perspective. "You have a job to do. I suggest you toughen your skin and stiffen your backbone."

"Why is it you can grant life-changing wishes, but you can't help me get Chase back or tell me who killed the fairy?"

"Because I'm the one who created this answer to your wish." She frowned and looked around. "Well, not exactly created. That was something that came from you. Possibly facilitated might be the right word."

"I don't understand the difference. What if I wish to be

with Chase right now?"

"I'm your fairy godmother, dear. If that is your wish, I shall make it come true."

"That is my wish," I reiterated. "I want to be with Chase right now."

There was no puff of smoke. No earthquake or high winds. I didn't even have to take a nap this time.

I was instantly with Chase in his dressing room—as he was getting ready to exercise his horse and practice for the joust. He had his shirt off and was changing pants.

He stood up straight. "Jessie! What are you doing here? Where did you come from?"

I was embarrassed and angry, but I knew I should make the most of the situation. It was unfortunate that I needed a shower and a change of clothes. I couldn't look less sexy if I'd tried.

"Sorry. I just needed a place to hang out for a while—until the bookstore opens." I tried not to stare at him. "I hope you don't mind."

He'd been facing the outside door to the dressing room so he knew I hadn't come in that way. Before he could ask, I told him that I'd been waiting for him.

"Why didn't you say something?" he questioned.

"I didn't want to embarrass you or make Isabelle jealous."

He laughed and finished changing. "Too late for that. Isabelle is jealous of every woman in the Village."

"I know." I hated to speak ill of the dead. Like Wanda, Isabelle was dead in my Village, but still alive here. "She knows you and I are just friends anyway, right?"

"She'll be fine." He sat in a chair to put on his boots. They were obviously new and stiff. "I wish I knew where my squire was. I spend more time looking for him than I do anything else."

It was a light bulb moment. I could literally feel the cartoon light going on above my head.

"I've been a squire before. I could be your new squire."

"I really don't think Isabelle would like that. But thanks for offering."

"No. Really." I dropped to the floor at his feet and took the boot from his hand. "I was a squire for Sir Mauny and Sir Reginald for a while. I'm very good, and discreet. I'll dress like a boy. No one will know it's me."

He stared down at me. "What about your apprenticeship?"

"I'm really not happy there." I'd never apprenticed with Paul Samuels anyway, so I had nothing to feel guilty about. "He's very impatient and sometimes downright mean. I'm stuck here for the rest of the summer. I have to do something to stay on the payroll."

"I don't know."

It only took me a moment to put on his boots. I brushed his doublet and handed him his sword. Maybe I wasn't very attractive at the moment, but I was useful.

"Please, Chase. You know I only come here to work on my dissertation over the summer. Don't make me go back early."

"Okay. But you'll have to dress appropriately for the field. Are you sure you want to do that?"

"With all my heart." I smiled, not getting too close to him. I could always do that later once I'd insinuated myself into his life—and had a bath. "Thanks. You won't be sorry."

"You couldn't be any worse. I'll see you later. The first joust is at eleven. Don't be late."

This wasn't the time to hug him. "Thank you. I'll be the best squire you ever had."

I left the dressing room before he did, hoping no one would see me and report back to Isabelle. I knew she had spies all over the Village. She'd always complained about losing Chase to me. Even in this muddled mess, she was bound to be angry if she learned I was working as his squire.

Halfway down the hill from the *Field of Honor*, Starshine appeared again.

"That wasn't what I meant about being with Chase, and

you knew it," I accused.

"Maybe not, but I'd say it worked out very well, wouldn't you?"

"Yes." I grinned. "It did, didn't it? I was thinking I could probably never duplicate that moment at the King's Feast when I believe we fell in love. I'll have to settle for this. I have the advantage of knowing how Chase feels about Isabelle. He didn't really love her, didn't even really like her. They just got along well . . . in other ways."

"You don't have to mince words with me, Jessie. I know all about the birds and the bees."

We walked along the cobblestones as I thought about what this was going to take.

"I have to get britches and a shirt from Portia. It won't be easy since she'll have me listed as working at the bookstore where I should be dressed in a peasant gown."

"I'm sure you'll find a way. But how will you get Chase involved in the murder investigation? Since he's not the Bailiff, he won't be part of it."

She was right, of course, but I thought I had the answer to that too.

"He'll be interested once I get some information about Apple Blossom. I know that much about him. Curiosity and wanting to take care of people was why he became Bailiff. If he wasn't here in the Village, I think he might've been a cop."

"Do you need me to do anything else?"

"No. Not right now. Maybe not ever unless you're going to reverse all this and put me back where I belong."

"Oh, of course not, dear. Where would be the learning experience in that? You'll be able to find all the answers you need. I'm going to rest for a while. I'll see you later."

I walked quickly toward the Main Gate. The Village was still closed, and things were quiet. I was too late to get a new costume which might have worked in my favor. The long line of residents waiting to get their clothes for the day was gone. That meant all the best costumes were gone with it.

"Jessie." Portia yawned, her face framed in the window at the costume shop. "It looks like you should have changed clothes yesterday. How are we supposed to get that clean for someone else?"

"I'm sure you can handle it, and you'll be glad to know that Paul wants me to clean up at the bookstore today, including his hand presses for creating the newspaper. He wants me to dress like a boy."

"Good idea," she said. "A gown is much harder to clean."

She reached behind her and grabbed a pair of heavy cotton britches and a blousy white shirt. "You'll have to make due with those boots you're wearing. I don't have any other in your size."

We both looked at my size twelve feet. I sighed, knowing I would have to wear damp boots all day. Portia turned away, finished with her part.

"Thanks." At least I was working on one of my goals, I reminded myself. I was going to get Chase back.

I spied Detective Almond was headed into the Village, no doubt to work on the fairy murder. Beside him was Officer Tom Grigg. In my Village, he'd been put in as an undercover cop and had gone native, becoming a pirate on the *Queen's Revenge*. It was so odd seeing him in uniform again. I followed them toward the *Good Luck Fountain*.

"Can I help you with something?" Detective Donald Almond asked after a short walk down the cobblestones.

It seemed he didn't know me either. Another casualty of my wish.

"I'm Jessie Morton," I told him. "I might be able to help you with your investigation into the fairy murder."

Detective Almond was nearly a foot shorter than me. He had a chubby face, and his pants were always too tight. He didn't have any food stains on his pale blue shirt yet, but the day was young.

"What do you know about it, Ms. Morton?"

"Not enough or I'd probably already have it solved," I

boasted. Maybe not a wise choice.

"Yeah?" He studied me. "How's that? Do you know who killed her?"

"No. Of course not. Not yet anyway."

"You're some kind of psychic, right? This place is full of crazies." He addressed the second half of his comment to Officer Grigg.

Grigg nodded, but didn't say anything.

"I'm not psychic. I do know a lot about the Village. I can tell that you're working with the wrong person."

"You mean Bailiff Britt?"

"Yes." I was inspired as I thought of a surefire way to bring Chase into the investigation. "You should talk to Chase Manhattan. He knows everyone in the Village and has a wonderful sense of right and wrong."

"So you're saying this Manhattan person knows about the fairy being killed?" Detective Almond's squinty eyes narrowed further on my face. "Are you trying to tell me he had something to do with it?"

"No. Of course not. I didn't say that. You misunderstood me." Was it too early to panic?

"Yeah. I get it." He nodded to Grigg. "Find the Bailiff. Have him bring Manhattan up here for questioning. Maybe now we're gonna get somewhere. Thanks, Ms. Morton."

Detective Almond started walking toward the Good Luck Fountain again.

Grigg was already heading toward the Dungeon.

What had I done? In my eagerness to involve Chase in this, I had implicated him in the murder.

Chapter Six

"Chase didn't kill the fairy." I stalked after Detective Almond with determination in my squelching boots and dirty dress. "I just meant he might have some insight into what happened."

"Look. You don't have to worry about it. I won't tell him where this came from. He'll never know you gave us his name."

"No. No. No." I put my hand on his arm to stop him. "You've got it all wrong."

"Are you saying you were part of it too? Is that how you know Manhattan was in on it?"

"Of course not. Chase would never kill a fairy or anyone else. I wouldn't help him either. I only meant that he knows his way around the Village and could be useful to you."

He grunted. "What does he do here?"

"He's a highly respected jouster on the Field of Honor

and Queen Olivia's favorite. Everyone loves him."

"A jouster, huh?" He glanced back at me as we reached the crime scene tape. "Funny that. The ME found traces of metal on the fairy's shoes. She was wearing those real pointy ones. He says she could've done some damage with those pointy toes. I wonder if she made some dents in Manhattan's armor."

I was horrified by this turn of events. I tried to think of something else to say that would take Chase out of the equation, but nothing came to mind. Maybe that was a good thing since it seemed I'd done such a bad job.

Grigg and Canyon approached with Chase between them a few minutes later. I panicked again when Chase looked squarely at me as though he knew what a mess I'd made of everything.

"You're Chase Manhattan?" Detective Almond leaned his head back to look up at him. "They make them big were you come from, huh? Where is that, by the way?"

"Arizona. But I haven't live there for years. I live here at the Village, at the castle."

Detective Almond's eyebrows went up and down rapidly. "So you're living the high life up there on the hill with the royals. What's that like?"

"It's all right." Chase glanced at me again. "Why am I here? Are you accusing me of something?"

"No. Just thinking we might have a conversation about someone named Apple Blossom."

"The dead fairy?"

"That's right. Your little girlfriend was right about you. You catch on fast."

What happened to keeping me out of it? So much for getting close to Chase by being his squire. He'd probably never forgive me if he thought I'd fingered him for Apple Blossom's killer.

Chase wasn't angry when he looked at me again—his dark eyes were betrayed and hurt.

"I didn't even know her," he told Detective Almond. "I

can't tell you anything about her or her death. You'll have to ask someone else."

"Okay. But I think I'll ask you a few more questions down at the station if that's okay." Detective Almond nodded to Grigg. "Another funny coincidence, Mr. Manhattan. The ME thinks whoever killed the fairy was a big, strong man like yourself. I'd say we have plenty to talk about."

Chase didn't offer any resistance to accompanying the police officers to their car. Grigg didn't put handcuffs on him. Detective Almond instructed Canyon to go through Chase's personal possessions and his jousting armor to search for anything that went along with the fairy's death.

"Yeah," Canyon complained when the police were gone with Chase. "Almond doesn't even have a search warrant. Guess who that will land on if Chase decides to press charges."

"I'm sure Detective Almond will get a search warrant for you."

What was I going to do to help Chase?

"Why were you up here while all this was going down, Jessie?" Canyon asked.

"I was on my way to work." I held up my small bag of clean clothes and didn't tell him that I was planning to work for Chase. I hoped he'd still have me when he got back. There was no doubt in my mind that the police wouldn't find anything to hold him.

"Good idea. I heard Paul was looking for you. The Main Gate will be open soon. In the meantime, I get stuck going through someone else's drawers."

Canyon asked me again about lunch. I turned him down again, though I planned to sneak back to the Dungeon and take a shower while he was busy. Getting naked with him there didn't sound like a good way to prepare him for our coming breakup.

Residents of the Village kept stopping me on the way to the Dungeon. They weren't interested in my love life anymore—they wanted to know if Chase had been arrested and what my part in it had been. I pushed away questions from everyone, including Merlin, who was also secretly the CEO of Adventure Land. He just liked living here.

I considered there might be some way to use that information to my advantage. Only a handful of people knew Merlin's true identity. Could I blackmail him into helping Chase?

A hundred thoughts fluttered through my mind like butterflies. Fairies and fire jugglers smiled at me as I walked by them. Mary, Mary Quite Contrary was selling vegetables from a cart along the way. Wandering minstrels were playing flutes and mandolins in the grass.

Finally at the Dungeon, I sneaked inside and ran up the stairs to the apartment. I locked both doors and got in the shower.

I thought about Chase and how we'd met, how we'd fallen in love. There had to be something in that knowledge that I could use.

It finally came to me. Detective Almond had taken me in for questioning in that other life. Chase and I had been friends but not yet lovers. He'd come to the police station to get me out of trouble.

Of course, he was a lawyer, if only a patent attorney. But no one had questioned that at the time. They'd believed he was my lawyer, and I'd left the station with him.

Could I pull that off?

It wasn't like Chase had ID that said he was a lawyer, right? He'd just had the panache to get in there when I needed him. I'd known him for a long time. But I hadn't known until then that he was a lawyer.

After my quick, hot shower, I rummaged through the drawers until I found my things. I had one good black suit and black heels that I'd always worn back to the university in Columbia when the summer was over. I found a pair of dark-rimmed glasses with only plain glass in them. I didn't recognize them so they might belong to Canyon. I took them anyway.

When I was dressed, I made sure my usual fly-away brown hair was under control, slicked back and professional-looking. I used a lot more makeup than I usually did and put the dark glasses on my face.

Wow. I didn't even look like myself. Could I convince Detective Almond that I was Chase's lawyer? I wouldn't know until I tried.

Dressed to kill, I walked down the cobblestones uncomfortably in my heels, stumbling every other step, focused on bringing Chase back to the Village.

I made it out of the Main Gate, going through the small employee's door on the side as visitors began to pour into the Village. In the parking lot I faced my greatest dilemma—this was the version of me that didn't have a car.

My heart sank like a stone in the sea of all my hopes.

Where was that pesky fairy godmother when I needed her?

I saw Chase's silver BMW, and my hopes rose again. Though I couldn't go to the castle and look for his keys, I knew where he kept a spare.

Bending carefully so I wouldn't mess up my skirt, I felt under the trunk, and there was his magnetic key holder. Flushed with success, I unlocked the car and got inside. I didn't think it would impress anyone at the police station that I was driving an expensive car that could belong to a lawyer, but it might impress Chase that I'd brought it to him.

Besides, I didn't want to ride the bus.

I'd driven the car a few times since we were married. It was simple to start and drive out of the parking lot. At every red light between the Village and the police station, I looked in the mirror and assured myself that I looked like a lawyer.

I would have Chase out of there in no time. It could be something wonderful as it had been when he'd rescued me and taken me in his arms.

The police station was in the same place. I parked at the curb, exactly where Chase had parked when he'd come to save me. I took a deep breath and adjusted my glasses.

Chase's briefcase was in the backseat, like always. I picked it up, got out, and locked the door.

I was going to get my man and bring him home.

Like many good resolutions, it was easier said than done.

The desk sergeant wanted to see my ID. I made a show of searching in the briefcase and then pretended to realize I'd left my pocketbook at home. It wasn't that hard. I was used to being different personalities at the Village. Pretending to be a lawyer wasn't a big deal. I talked with the woman at the front desk. She was very understanding.

Besides, if I wasn't Chase's lawyer, how would I know he was there?

In the end, despite a mini interrogation by Detective Almond—who didn't recognize me—they weren't going to arrest Chase anyway. When they were finished questioning him, I walked in with the briefcase looking serious and ready to stand my ground.

It had been different when Chase had come for me. He had ID and dramatically broke into my interview with Detective Almond. They weren't holding me that day either, but I'd been scared and alone. It had been wonderful to see his friendly face.

Unfortunately, he wasn't wearing his friendly face when I walked into the interrogation room. He was gathering his ID and getting ready to leave. I smiled when he looked up.

He glanced away with a frown. "What do you want, Jessie? Haven't you done enough damage for today?"

No pulling me into his arms as his hero or rushing to commend me on how clever I was to find a way to help him.

"I came to get you out."

"They never planned on arresting me. Thanks anyway." He stared hard at the briefcase. "Is that mine?"

"Yes. I thought it would add to the effect. I'm supposed to be a lawyer—your lawyer. I knew you needed someone. I was the best person for the job."

"Maybe next time it would be better not to incriminate me to the investigating officer in the first place," he suggested, picking up his briefcase.

"That's not what I meant when I talked to him, Chase."

"That's the way he took it, Jessie."

He walked out of the room, past the curious stares of the police officers. He was still wearing his tight leather Ren Faire clothes and boots.

I followed quickly behind him, trying to maintain my persona as his legal defense. The desk sergeant smiled and waved as I walked out the front door. At least I'd made one friend.

Chase stopped abruptly when he saw his BMW parked outside the station.

"Did you drive this here?"

"Yes. I know where you keep your spare key. I've driven your car before."

He wasn't impressed. If anything, he was angrier. "How did you know about my key? And what do you mean you've driven my car? Are you stalking me? Is that why you want to be my squire?"

"No. This is getting completely messed up." I bit my lip, trying to think what I could say to bring him over to my side. Maybe I shouldn't have told him about driving the car. I just thought he might feel like he could trust me.

"Did you kill that fairy, and you're trying to blame it on me? Is this whole thing a setup?" He ran his hand through his long brown hair. "You started this right after the fairy died. Everyone knows how you feel about fairies. It's no secret."

Really? Even in this place everyone knew I hated fairies? I didn't think I'd started hating them until after Chase and I were together. They were always flitting around him and flirting. I thought that was the beginning. Apparently I was wrong.

To make matters worse, Princess Isabelle drove up in one of those red mini-cars. Her long black hair was perfectly sleek against her head, and her pale mauve dress was exactly what someone would wear to save their lover who was in jail.

"Chase!" She left her car in the street and ran up to join

us, but she was staring at me as she wound her arms, and her lithe body, around him

"It's okay, Isabelle. I'm fine."

"Who is she?" Her eyes narrowed on my face like daggers.

"This is my public defender," Chase answered to my complete surprise. "She got me out of jail."

I smiled, cool and professional, the way I'd practiced in the car mirror on the way to the police station. I held out my hand to her in a totally objective way. "Jessica."

"Thank you." She barely touched her cool white hand to mine before turning back to Chase.

But that was all that mattered. She'd bought it.

What I couldn't figure out was why Chase had helped me sell it to her. It had to be that he didn't want her to be jealous. I didn't even sneak a glance at him in case it all fell apart.

"Isn't this your car?" Isabelle asked him.

"Yeah. They let me drive myself here. They aren't charging me with anything. They just had a few questions."

"Well. Good, I guess." She shrugged. "I wish I'd known. There was no reason for me to come running over here. I guess I'll see you at home."

Chase and I watched her leave. When her cute little car was gone, I realized I was about to get hit with an avalanche of anger from my companion. It was so unfair since he loved me and not Isabelle.

"Let's go," he said. "I'll drive, if you don't mind."

I handed him the keys. "I'm sorry. I was just trying to make everything right."

He walked toward the car. "Don't worry about it. I know you, Jessie. You wouldn't have done this on purpose. I'm sorry I said that to you before. I've just had a bad day."

"Thanks. I'll make it up to you."

"Yes, you will. As my squire, you and I are going to figure out who killed the fairy."

Chapter Seven

The Village was open when we got back. The parking lot was full to overflowing, hundreds more visitors still putting on their costumes as they took them from their cars.

Our conversation hadn't been much coming from the police department. Chase spent the whole time explaining to me why we were going to have to find Apple Blossom's killer. Despite the way he looked (hot) and his job as Bailiff (exciting) he can be more boring than any college professor.

And I didn't care. The whole thing had worked out to my benefit. He wanted me to help him figure out who did it. That was exactly what Starshine had said I needed. I was feeling triumphant.

"I hope you got the right costume from Portia this morning," he said. "Our joust is in fifteen minutes. Make sure you're there."

"I will." I closed the car door and walked quickly

through the employee's gate.

"I'd say you made real progress with Chase." Starshine ambushed me as I entered the Village. "That was a brilliant plan, Jessie."

"Thanks," I muttered. "I didn't know if it would work, but we're okay. At least on the murder investigation part. I'm not sure about being his love interest, but I'm working on that. At least he forgave me for putting him into the middle of the investigation."

She giggled and kicked her tiny feet as she buzzed along beside me. Lucky for me that half the people in the Village talked to themselves or some imaginary person most of the time. No one paid any attention.

"You were right to send me to Chase's dressing room, even though it was embarrassing. This way I'm his squire, and squires do some pretty intimate stuff for their jousters. I think this could work."

"I'm sure it will. Just be careful. Once you and Chase begin asking questions in the Village, you could be in danger. Someone killed Apple Blossom. He or she might come after you."

"Thanks. This isn't my first rodeo. I can handle myself." I glanced at my watch. "I have to run. Chase needs me at the Field of Honor in a few minutes. I hope I can sneak in and out of the Dungeon without running into Canyon."

"I'm sure I can grant that wish."

As I blinked my eyes, I was inside the apartment in the Dungeon. I glanced around, getting my bearings after my abrupt move from the parking lot. There was no sign of Canyon. I immediately started changing clothes.

"Surprise!" Canyon put his hands over my eyes. "We're both here at the same time. It doesn't get much better than that. Looks like you were thinking what I was thinking—let's get naked and have some fun."

I pushed him away, but I did it with a smile. "I'm so late for work. I have to go."

"Come on, Jessie. You're always in such a hurry. I know

that Paul Samuels fired you today and got another apprentice. You can't hide the big, important things from me. I'm the Bailiff. I know everything that goes on here."

I stripped off my jacket but didn't dare remove any more unless I wanted to end up in bed with him. "Did you get those reports from Detective Almond?"

"Yes." He sighed impatiently. "They're on the table."

I grabbed the few clothes I had there and shoved them into a tote bag with the reports. This time wasn't real anyway, at least not if I could change it. What difference did it make what else I left behind?

"How about your search through Chase's things? How did that go?"

"Not much. If he killed the fairy, he hid it well. Why are you so interested?" He cocked his head to the side. "You do have a thing for Manhattan, don't you? You're dumping me."

"I'm sorry, Canyon. I'm sure it's been fun, although I can't recall any of it. But yes. I love Chase, and I'm going to work for him as his squire. I'll get the rest of my stuff later."

"You can't dump me." He grabbed my arm. "Girls don't dump me. I dump them."

I could see his blue eyes were serious despite his crazy words.

"If it makes you feel any better, you can dump me. Or at least tell everyone that you dumped me. I don't care."

"What about Princess Isabelle? Chase isn't gonna leave anyone that fine and lose his place at the castle. You're dreaming, Jessie. You better wake up before it's too late."

"Thanks for the tip. I'll see you around."

I was quickly out the door, tote in hand. I realized I was faced with the dilemma of where I could change clothes. I barely had time to make it to the *Field of Honor* before Chase was ready for the joust. Tony's place was on the other side of the Village. I wouldn't make it there and back in time.

Starshine wasn't around to wish me into my squire's clothes and up to the Field of Honor, so I had to run down the cobblestones. It only took a minute for me to realize that my heels weren't going to make it. I shed them in the trashcan as I went past the tree swing that was between the Dungeon and the privies.

"Run, Jessie, run!" Merlin encouraged in his star-studded purple robe. He held his wizard's hat on his head to keep the wind from blowing it away.

"I wish you were a real wizard," I said before I realized what the words could mean. "Just kidding. I don't really wish that at all, if you're listening. Cross that one out."

My feet were sore by the time I'd reached the *Field of Honor*. I ignored them. My soggy boots were at the Dungeon. I had big feet for a woman, but Chase's feet were much larger so I couldn't borrow boots from him. I was going to have to be a shoeless squire.

He wasn't in his dressing room when I got there. *Huzzah!* I immediately stripped down to my underwear and started putting on my britches and shirt.

"I guess you got here just in time," he said from behind me.

What was it with men sneaking up on me? First Canyon and then Chase. Not that I minded Chase seeing me in my pretty pink bra and panties. After all, getting him to notice me was a big part of what I was doing.

"Sorry. I've got clothes. I just needed somewhere to change, and Tony's place is all the way over on the other side."

I purposely put on the blousy white top most people wore in the Village and left it open while I pulled up the britches. The pants were a tight fit—what was Portia thinking? But I got them fastened and was happy to see that Chase was still staring at me. I left the shirt open more than usual.

"You need your armor." I fetched it from the spot where he'd left it after the last joust. It hadn't been cleaned, but it was going to have to do.

I picked up the breast plate and fastened it on him. He wore light chain mail under it, on top of his shirt. There were many times when the fake jousts got a little too real, and jousters were most vulnerable in the chest area.

"Let me get your helmet," I said. "Sorry this is such a rush job. I'll have your armor shining before the next match."

"Where are your shoes?" He glanced at my feet.

"I had to ditch the heels and forgot the boots." I shrugged. "I'll be fine. It's just dirt and sand."

"And heavy hoofs," he added. "Find something you can wear. I don't want you to get hurt."

"I won't." I handed him his gauntlets. "You have to be on the field right now. Let me worry about my feet. Good luck."

There wasn't time to ask the other squires if they had any smaller boots they could loan me. I got Chase out of the dressing room and on his horse before I handed him his sword. His lances would be out on the field. I'd give them to him as needed.

He was jousting against Sir Reginald, one of the older knights who was a royal favorite. He was the only knight who lived at the castle besides Chase. In my Village, he'd had a heart attack after jousting with Chase and had gone into semi-retirement, working as a sort of majordomo at the castle. His daughter actually became the first female jouster—a title I had coveted years before but had been denied.

Of course that didn't seem to be the case now. There sat Sir Reginald beside the grandstand, his squire carrying his standard.

I grabbed Chase's standard on my way to the field. It held a great lion on a field of green. I pushed it into his station where I would wait for him and his lances were kept.

Our side of the field was full with spectators who shouted *Huzzah!* loudly as he took the field. He held his broadsword before him and smiled into the sun. He never put on his helm, as Sir Reginald had, until his fans had a chance to see his face.

Chase's cheerleader was more focused on watching him

than leading her spectators to boo his opponent. She was besotted like all the other females, including me. Even Sir Reginald's cheerleader had accidentally led her people into cheering for Chase.

This wasn't the King's or Queen's Joust, so neither of them was present in the grandstands. I saw Princess Isabelle up there with her court of followers. Her eyes were pinned on me instead of Chase.

I wasn't wearing the dark-rimmed glasses, but it was still likely that she recognized me from the police station. That meant she would give Chase hell when they saw each other again in private. I was sorry for that, in a way. On the other hand, I planned to steal him from her as I had years before in my Village. Maybe this was a way to let her know I was after him.

Lord Dunstable was still dropping the kerchief to begin the joust from the grandstand. Another older knight, he only performed this function at the King's Feast in my world, but I understood he'd once done it at every joust in the Village. Strange, the things that were the same and those that were different. How much was affected by my wish for Chase not to be Bailiff?

There was no time to ruminate over the answers. I handed Chase his helm and took the sword from him. I gave him a lance and then stepped back. My feet were killing me on the rough mixture of sand, gravel, and dirt. Even the hay poked into them.

Chase was a strong jouster. Very few knights could stand against him. He'd started jousting right out of college when he'd first come to the Village. At the time, it had been the only thing he wanted to do.

The jousts were partially real in that two men on horses went at each other quickly with pointed objects in their hands. The lances were thin and mostly gave way when they hit an opponent. Sometimes there were injuries, usually from jousters falling from their mounts.

I shuddered in this case to imagine Chase knocking poor

Sir Reginald from his horse. He wasn't exactly elderly, but he wasn't in great condition like the younger knights. Who'd set this up anyway? Even though this was a different Village, I wondered if this was the time that Sir Reginald would have a heart attack.

How could I watch and let this happen?

Answer—I couldn't. It wasn't me.

"Wait! Stop!" I ran between the two men, yelling and screaming like a banshee, waving my arms around. "Don't joust."

Sir Reginald's horse reared up, and he lost his seat. He tumbled to the ground, but wasn't hurt.

"You must curb your squire, Sir Knight." His voice was loud enough to make a spectacle of it.

That was the whole point in being here.

People booed and yelled for me to leave the field. Chase stared down at me.

"What are you at, squire? Back to the station with you before I give you a good hiding."

"Please, good Sir Knight." I got on my knees and raised my hands to him in supplication. "Do not harm the ancient, frail knight. Allow him to go back to the castle in dignity and peace."

"What?" Sir Reginald sounded amazed, his voice echoing from behind his helm.

Cheerleaders and spectators laughed like it was the funniest thing they'd ever heard. I didn't care. Sir Reginald had almost died in my Village, and Chase had felt bad for weeks. There was no reason it should happen here. I could stop it.

"Get that varlet off the field," the older knight sneered.

His cheerleader took up the chant, encouraging his fans to follow her. "Off the field. Off the field."

I put my hand on Chase's knee—that was as high as I could reach with him on horseback. "Please don't let him joust."

He raised his visor. His dark eyes were confused and

curious. Yet as he was about to speak, a large cloud came up and began raining hard on us. There were deafening thunderclaps and strong winds that blew many of the banners down.

Spectators and Village residents ran to shelter. Sir Reginald's horse bolted toward the stables. I didn't move, wondering if this was the work of my fairy godmother. It seemed well-planned to me. Then lightning struck where Sir Reginald had been standing only a moment before. He was much faster getting off the field than I'd anticipated.

"I guess you get your wish," Chase said. "Come on. Get up here."

He put his hand down and pulled me on the back of his horse. We rode past his station, and I picked up his sword. I knew how important it was, made just for him.

After that, we got off the field and past the grandstand. The red and green bunting looked bedraggled in the rain. I could feel Isabelle's eyes boring holes in me. I hoped she'd only continue being threatening without any physical complications until this was over. She had a nasty slap and sharp nails. Kind of like fighting a pretty cat.

We got off the horse in the stable as four or five other knights and jousters were leaving in disgust. Squires ran to take care of their wet animals. I knew Chase would expect the same of me—happily, no doubt, since I'd interrupted the joust.

"Be sure there's fresh hay for him," he instructed. "And get back to the dressing room right away. I thought you knew what you were doing out there. Squires don't interrupt jousts."

I was about to attempt some kind of explanation. He saved me from my whirling thoughts that made absolutely no sense. "Jessie, your feet are bleeding. I told you to find some shoes."

"There isn't exactly a shoe store in your dressing room," I tartly reminded him. So that was why my feet hurt so much. "I can't wear your boots. I know my feet probably look big enough, but they aren't."

"Whatever," he growled. "Here, boy!" He called to a young knave sheltering in the barn from the storm. "Dry my horse and I'll give you ten dollars."

"*Huzzah!*" the young man yelled and took the horse's reins.

I didn't know why Chase was giving the boy my job. Did that mean he was done with me? I couldn't believe I'd messed up my advantage being his squire because of Sir Reginald. I'd never even liked him. He was always so pompous and self-important.

"Let's get back to the dressing room."

"Chase, I—"

He bent slightly and lifted me in his arms like he'd always done, as though I weighed nothing.

"You can't walk until we take care of your feet," he said. "Just be quiet and hang on while I gallantly resist dropping you in the horse trough. What was up with you out there anyway?"

Isabelle was standing in front of us. "You know, Chase, I think the squire is supposed to care for the knight."

Chapter Eight

"She's hurt." Chase turned me so she could see my dirty, bleeding feet.

"I don't care if she has a sword in her chest." She glared at me. "She can walk. Put her down."

"Isabelle, there's nothing going on between us." Chase smiled at her. "I'd do the same if she was a boy squire."

"Well she's not. People are talking. You know how I hate that." She pouted prettily. "Let someone else take care of her, please."

"I've already got her. I'm taking her back to my dressing room. You can come with us to chaperone if you like. Nothing is going to happen. Don't worry so much."

She glared at both of us and gritted her teeth, snapping at her attendants as a dozen parasols went up to protect her from the rain.

Chase glanced at me and sighed. "She'll be okay. You

know how she is."

I did know how she was, and I knew this wouldn't be the end of it. But for the moment, I was in his arms, and I meant to take full advantage of the situation. I slid my arms around his neck and pressed close to him.

"Uh, Jessie, you're not getting the wrong idea, are you?" he asked as he walked toward the dressing room in the drizzle.

"No. I just don't want you to drop me. I'm not exactly a lightweight."

"You're not a heavyweight either." He grinned. "Can you open the door?"

I opened the door with a sweet smile. He plunked me down in a chair.

"Don't move. Let me get my first aid kit. I can't believe you were out there with your feet like this."

"I'm your squire." I made sure our eyes were on the same level. "I'd do anything for you."

He looked skittish at that and mumbled something about finding boots before he left the dressing room. I sighed and sat back in the chair.

Ten minutes later, he was back. I loved him so much when he pulled up a short stool and first washed the bottom of my feet and then added some kind of liniment. He wouldn't have had to work so hard—just looking at him made me feel better all over.

"These aren't exactly regulation Ren wear." He put white socks on my feet. "But you'll probably need them with the boots."

I came out of my Chase-induced love haze and realized I needed to move forward with the plan. "I have the police report about the fairy's death. And I know they didn't find anything incriminating when they searched your room at the castle."

"Thanks. I'm not sure about following through on looking for the killer," he said as he put on the half-boots that were common for peasants to wear. "If I'm in the clear, I guess it doesn't matter."

"But what if you don't stay in the clear?" Thank goodness I'd brought it up. "Detective Almond is like a dog with a bone when he gets an idea. He isn't going to stop watching you. We have to fight back, and the only way is to find the killer."

"You're very passionate about it," he said. "How well do you know Detective Almond? I never met him before today. Canyon takes care of all that stuff."

"I know." *Forgive me one little white lie.* "But he thinks you might be guilty too. You read the ME's description of the killer. It was someone strong enough to strangle the fairy with one hand while he held her underwater."

"Yeah." Chase wiped off his hands on a towel. "I guess you're right. There was also the part about the fairy kicking the armor. That had to be a knight or one of the jousters. It could be me—or about a dozen other people—including Canyon. Maybe that's why the Bailiff thinks I did it. He wants to throw suspicion off himself."

He was finally intrigued by the situation. I'd seen it on his face a hundred times as we searched for someone who stole money from the Brotherhood of the Sheaf, an antique teapot from the *Honey and Herb Shoppe*, or a valuable glass statue from the *Glass Gryphon*. I could see he was on the trail.

"Let me get the report and you can look through it, just like old times." *Oops.* The words were out before I could stop them.

Chase had been unbuckling his breast plate. He paused to stare at me.

"What? We've never done anything like this. Is there something about me that reminds you of Canyon?" He laughed so I knew it was okay.

I got the report out of my bag. My feet really felt a lot better. Chase had been a paramedic for a while after college. It was partially that experience that had made Adventure Land hire him as the Bailiff.

After he'd taken off his armor, I handed him a cold ale from the mini-fridge and gave him the police report. As he read it and relaxed, I cleaned his boots and polished his armor. I tidied up the room and finally paused to see how he was taking it.

"She was only twenty." He shook his head. "If someone who lives in the Village is responsible, you're right. We have to find him."

Yes! The plan is in play.

He glanced at his watch. "Are your feet okay?"

"They're fine. Don't worry about them."

"Good. We've got a few hours before the next joust. Let's see what we can find out. Residents who live and work around the Good Luck Fountain are going to be more likely to talk to us instead of the police. That's our advantage."

"I'm ready to go."

He handed me the file. "Just remember to walk a few paces behind me in public and don't speak unless I speak to you first. We have roles to play."

Ugh. I'd forgotten that part of being a squire or a servant.

Still it was better to be with Chase than hang around the Village without him. The murder investigation was getting started. I just needed to ramp up my romantic assault.

We walked through the Village with everyone hailing Chase as we passed *Frenchy's Fudge Shoppe* and the *Pleasant Pheasant*, a tavern close to the Dungeon.

Canyon came out as we were going by. I hoped he wouldn't make a big deal out of me working for Chase, but I didn't really know him, or his responses, in either Village.

"What ho, Sir Knight," Canyon greeted Chase but his eyes were on me. "It appears that you have a new squire."

"Good morrow to you, Sir Bailiff," Chase returned. "Yes. She is all that I could ask for in a servant."

Cameras flashed as visitors on the cobblestones began to sense a Renaissance throw-down.

"And a prime bit of flesh she is too, sir." Canyon put his

hand on my butt and squeezed.

Maybe if we had really been lovers, I might have let that go, even though we were in public with pictures likely to end up on the Internet. But we weren't lovers—not even friends. I barely knew him.

My intentions must have been obvious as I turned to him. Chase put his hand out before I could sink my knee into Canyon's groin.

"Allow me, fair squire." He bowed graciously to me, although a knight would never have done such a thing with a servant.

As dozens of residents and visitors watched, Chase slapped Canyon and then dropped one of his gloves on the ground. It was a challenge to a duel if Canyon picked it up.

My imaginary ex didn't hesitate. He lifted Chase's glove. "I believe that makes the choice of weapons mine, sir. My second will contact you."

Both men nodded curtly at each other and set off in opposite directions.

The crowd went wild. Applause and camera flashes followed for at least five minutes until there was something else new and exciting to look at.

"You didn't have to do that," I whispered as we walked away. "I could've handled it without a duel."

"Are you speaking to me, squire? I don't believe I've spoken to you."

"You know, he's really good with a sword." I didn't really know that. I was just trying to protect him in case it was true. "That's the weapon he'll choose."

Chase grinned. "That's what I was hoping for. I'm not so bad with a sword myself."

He was right, of course. He was very good with a sword. I'd never seen Canyon fight, so I didn't know how good he was. That made me nervous. Not that they'd be fighting to the death or anything. But there were always accidents. And what if Canyon was really the fairy killer and wanted to get Chase out of the way so he could frame him for the murder?

We continued down the cobblestones to the Village Square. Detective Almond and Officer Grigg were already there. Chase had me wait at one of the benches, away from the fountain. He held out his hand to Detective Almond, already getting to know him.

"You've had a busy morning but well-played, my dear." Starshine appeared on the bench beside me. "I might've used him working on your feet a little more to your advantage." She shrugged and giggled. "But it went very well. He cares for you. That is obvious. He's even willing to make his girlfriend angry for you. You and Chase are well on your way to a more personal relationship."

"It might be better if Canyon went away," I mumbled, hoping she might take that as a wish without me actually wishing it.

"I can't remove him, dear. You brought him into this whole thing. He'll remain through it."

"Is he the killer?"

"How should I know? I'm sure it won't be long and you and Chase will have figured out the whole thing."

She vanished abruptly as Chase came near.

"Detective Almond is a hard nut to crack." He sat on the bench with me. "I thought I might get him to warm up. No luck. At least I have his report. Thanks, Jessie."

"You're welcome. What do we do now?"

"Now we strike out on our own. The report says the fairy was killed as the Village was closing. That means most visitors were still here. I'm not sure how we're going to be able to tell if it was a visitor or a resident that killed her."

"Do you think it was a resident?"

"Detective Almond does." Chase nodded toward him. "Let's investigate that idea first. We both know most visitors who wear armor during the summer don't make it through the whole day which probably means the killer is a resident."

I glanced around the Village Square located in the center of the King's Highway. I knew this area so well I could have told anyone what shops were around it.

There was the *Romeo and Juliet Pavilion*, where two pretty actors repeated words from the Shakespearian play a hundred times every day. There was *Fractured Fairy Tales*, which were storytellers with a more random, sometimes ribald, point of view on Cinderella, Snow White, and other well-known tales.

Close by, within viewing distance of the fountain, was also the well of the *Lovely Laundry Ladies* who washed their clothes in public and traded insults and sexy innuendoes with visitors. On the other side of the square was the *Treasure Trove Shop* and *Leather and Lace*, a shop for more adventurous clothing buyers.

"Someone in one of those places may have seen what went down here," Chase said. "It seems more likely to me that it could be the Fairy Tales or Romeo and Juliet since they have no walls."

"Let's start there," I agreed. "I'll be a few paces behind you in deferential servitude, of course, Sir Knight."

"Of course." He held his head regally high.

We hadn't gone far toward the *Romeo and Juliet Pavilion* when Sir Reginald stepped out to face Chase down about what had happened at the joust. He still wore his red and green jousting doublet and dark hose with knee-high boots.

"I demand an explanation. Why did you let your squire halt the joust this morning?"

Chase glanced at me, but this was one time I chose to keep quiet. Maybe he could think of a better explanation than that my feet hurt. I surely couldn't tell Sir Reginald that I was afraid he might have a heart attack.

"My squire was taken ill, sir," Chase said. "She didn't mean to stop the joust, although it would have been called a moment later with the storm anyway."

"That's not good enough, sir!" He was so angry that his hands were trembling.

I was afraid all over again that he might fall down dead at our feet. He'd recovered in the other Village, but what if this one was different? I knew he couldn't take the stress.

"I can't offer any better explanation." Chase's reply was calm as he stared into Sir Reginald's rapidly reddening face.

The older jouster pulled out a red leather glove and slapped Chase in the face with it.

"You may call on my seconds, sir, as to your choice of weapon!"

"Oh brother," Chase muttered as Sir Reginald imperiously stalked away.

Chapter Nine

I couldn't believe Sir Reginald had challenged Chase to a duel right after Chase had challenged Canyon. It was crazy.

Of course the king and queen had the last word on any duels set in the Village. The duels weren't real, but staging would be required to make them appear so. Hardly anything happened to us personally that couldn't be used to promote the Village.

"What are you going to do?" I was glad that my long legs helped me keep up with Chase's angry pace.

"Fight Sir Reginald if I have to. I'm hoping Queen Olivia won't allow it."

Even in this Village, Chase was the queen's favorite. She'd probably put an end to it, even though it was staged.

He kept walking until we'd reached the *Romeo and Juliet Pavilion*, which was more like a garden bower decked with roses and lilies. There were two chaise lounges at the

center of it for the actors, and chairs around the circle for the
visitors. The roses and lilies were real during the summer—
fake in the winter.

People loved the romantic performance. There were
always tears and sighs when the couple was both dead. Not
much of a romance to my mind. I didn't want my romance
with Chase to end that way.

There was applause from the tearful visitors as beautiful
Juliet and handsome Romeo were laid out together at the end.
As the performance ended, the visitors began to look at their
Village maps for their next destination.

Chase waited until the couple was alone and drinking
water from the canteens that were allowed in the Village.
There were no plastic water bottles here—at least not for
residents.

"Warren." Chase shook his hand. "Nice performance.
How many times a day are you doing this now?"

Sexy, dark-eyed, dark-haired Warren wiped his sweaty
brow with a towel. "Too many. I requested a transfer to the
castle. Who is your lovely squire?" He kissed my hand. "Hi
there, cutie."

"Sorry," Chase said. "Squires can't speak unless their
masters speak to them."

"As it should be," Fake Juliet said in a waspish tone.
"What do you want, Chase? We're kind of busy here. Of
course we would be even busier if Warren quit messing up
his lines."

"Me? I've never worked with a worse actress than you,
Paulette. And forget the kissing. I'd rather kiss a rock."

Before the couple could erupt into full civil war, I broke
in. "We were wondering if you saw anything unusual the
evening that the fairy was killed."

Chase glared at me for talking out of turn, but in another
minute, there wouldn't have been time before the next show
to ask them anything.

Warren took my hand again. "She speaks! The angel has
a voice of a thousand church bells."

"Okay." Chase put a stop to the effusive compliments. "I'll punish her later. Did either of you see anything unusual?" Paulette drank some water and used a towel to carefully dab perspiration from her face. "I think she was already dead when we got finished. Warren and I thought she was sick. From here it looked like she was leaning over the edge of the fountain instead of drowning in it. Sorry we can't help."

"She's right," Warren agreed. "Who'd do something like this with thousands of visitors wandering around the Village? He had to be cold, that's for sure."

"Or sure of himself," Paulette added. "Crazy things go on here every day. I thought Lorenzo had killed Diego the other day. Unless you were paying very close attention, anyone might have thought she was sick like we did."

"Wish we could help," Warren said. "I don't like the idea that someone was killed right in our own backyard. Have you talked to Merlin? I remember seeing him out there that day. Maybe he noticed something."

Chase thanked them and wished Warren good luck with his new job. We walked away as the audience was already starting to fill up again.

"You're not going by the squire's code," he reminded me.

"You were waiting too long. They only have short breaks."

"I think there's a rule against squires arguing with their masters too."

He grinned as he said it. He was joking, but I knew a few knights and royal personages who had very strict rules for their servants.

"Well I'm walking behind you," I observed. "That might be the best you're going to get. Unless you need a massage after a joust. I'm very good with my hands."

It was suggestive for both a friend and a squire. His eyes darkened in surprise, and then he looked away.

Score one for me!

We reached the *Fractured Fairy Tales Pavilion*, but they were in the middle of their weird, R-rated rendition of the Goldilocks and the Three Bears. The audience laughed loudly as Papa Bear took Goldilocks over his knee.

"We'll talk to them later," Chase decided. "It's almost lunchtime. Let's see if we can catch someone at *Leather and Lace* after lunch."

"Where are you planning to eat?" I casually questioned.

"I always have lunch with Isabelle," he said. "I'd invite you to eat with us, but I don't think it's going to be a pleasant experience."

"That's okay." It certainly wouldn't be a pleasant experience for me, though I hated to give her the time alone with him. "I'll get lunch somewhere and meet you after."

We decided to meet back at the Good Luck Fountain and start from there again. Chase was apologetic that he had to leave me. I assured him that I would be fine.

I got some free lemonade from one of the vendors and talked another into giving me a free pretzel. I'd come to this strange place without any money. Not even a voucher that employees received for food and drinks.

Hundreds of fairies, knaves, varlets, and high-born ladies and gentlemen walked around the Village Green as near to the closed off fountain as they possibly could without touching it. They muttered to each other, very few knowing what had happened. I felt sorry for Apple Blossom, even though she was a fairy. I opened the file and stared at the picture of her.

She was very pretty, dressed in apple green with a crown of tiny green apples and leaves on her brown hair. This wasn't the picture of her that the police had taken after her death. This was better times, with a friend who was also dressed as a fairy. The second fairy was wearing dark purple and had a blueberry crown on her dirty blond hair.

It must've been a fruit fairy thing.

When I looked up, the blueberry fairy from the picture

was standing very close to the police tape. She was crying—her nose and eyes were red. She was still in her purple fairy garb that appeared to be made of leaves sewn together. It barely reached her thighs.

I had to put aside my hostility at fairies not having to observe the same Ren Faire protocol as the rest of us. Being angry didn't serve any of my plans to get back to my Village. But being nice to the crying fairy just might.

"I'm so sorry." I towered over her, resisting the urge to slump. "I'm Jessie. I work for the Village. It was a terrible tragedy what happened to your friend."

She didn't question how I knew about Apple Blossom—it was enough that I worked for the Village. My words brought out a full storm of tears that she cried against my blouse.

By walking slowly to the bench where I'd been sitting, I got her to follow me.

"My name is Stacie, but my fairy name is Blueberry. You're so kind to take an interest in what happened to Apple Blossom." She was trying to pull herself together, pain in her hazel eyes. "I don't think the police took her death seriously. They barely questioned anyone."

"Believe me, the police take it very seriously, and so does the Village Bailiff, Chase Manhattan. I work for him." The words just came out without much thought behind them.

"The Bailiff?" Her eyes were enormous in her pale face. "Wow! Apple Blossom had a crush on him. I kind of do too. All that leather . . . and I love his hair!"

"Yes." I gritted my teeth. "He has very nice hair."

"He could lock me in his Dungeon anytime"

I ignored her ramblings about him. "The evidence is very compelling that she was murdered."

"Murdered?" Her pale brows knit together. "I'll bet it was that big man who followed us around the Village. He kept stopping and talking to us. He wanted Apple Blossom to go out with him. He'd asked her before today, but today he was really annoying. He was like a hundred years old, but he had a nice costume, and he wasn't bad looking—except for being old."

Maybe now we were getting somewhere. "What exactly did he look like?"

"I don't know. He was just old and big."

No point in asking if she'd told the police. What would they say to such a vague description?

"What about his costume?" That was something Detective Almond wasn't very good at. If it related to anything only found at the Village, he acted as though he couldn't understand it.

"Oh." She thought hard about his clothes. "He was dressed like someone with money. Maybe a lord or a king. I think he was mostly wearing red and black. Oh! And he wore gloves and matching boots."

I wrote what she said on one of the papers in the file.

"Anything else? Was he dark-haired? Fair? Did you hear him speak?"

"I heard him speak. There wasn't anything different about it. He wasn't British or anything like Wanda. He had dark hair, like Chase, but maybe not so long. He wore a short sword. That's all I can remember."

"Thanks." I put the stubby pencil in the leather bag tied around my waist, next to my cup for free drinks. "I'm sure this will be helpful."

"I hope you catch him." She started crying again. "Apple Blossom was like my sister, only better, because my sister is completely stupid and I hate her."

"We'll be in touch, Blueberry Fairy."

"Blueberry. Or Stacie." She corrected her name. "Thank you."

She stood at the fountain again for a while and looked so forlorn that I really felt sorry for her. A few other fruit fairies joined her—cherry, peach, and orange.

I thought about her description of the man who might have killed Apple Blossom. Too bad that description fit so many men wandering around the Village. It could even have been Chase. No wonder Detective Almond had questioned him.

Robin Hood and his Merry Men were reenacting their daily show of chasing the Sheriff of Nottingham out of Sherwood Forest.

I wasn't sure what the Village personnel director had been thinking when he'd hired the new sheriff. He was short and thin, wore glasses, and apparently didn't ride a horse, although that was usual to this skit.

In contrast, Robin and his men were tall and brawny. They didn't ride horses either, which was just as well. It would've looked as though they were bullying the sheriff if they had. The new sheriff kept running down the cobblestones toward the other end of the Village as Robin did his famous laugh and the audience applauded.

Even when the skit was over, the sheriff was still running. It looked as though they might need a new sheriff.

Chase was back from lunch—with Isabelle clinging to him like a side-saddle. My hopes for our continued relationship plummeted.

"Jessie." He was upbeat about her presence—ridiculously so. "Isabelle is going to help us with the investigation."

"So you're not needed, squire." She smiled at me. "You can go back to the stables and shine Chase's armor."

"We talked about this," Chase said to her. "Jessie is helping. She can shine armor later."

"But that was before I was here, baby." She put her hand on his chest. "We don't need her now."

"I need her. She's my squire. I only have about an hour until the next joust. She stays." His decision was surprisingly forceful.

I really wanted to stick my tongue out at her when Chase's back was turned, but I didn't do it. Instead I told him what the blueberry fairy had said about her friend. He said the same thing about her description matching a hundred men in the Village.

"Let's take up our quest and go to *Leather and Lace*," he suggested. "Maybe they have a lead on the older man wearing red."

"Sounds like Santa," Isabelle purred and snuggled up to him.

Chase and I both ignored her, but she held his arm as we went into the Renaissance clothing store.

It was very dark in the small building. Candles burned from sconces on the walls. It would've been this way if it had been the 1500s. Despite the bright sunlight outside, there were very few windows. They were mostly too expensive for small businesses or poor people.

The owner of *Leather and Lace* greeted Chase with a hearty handshake. Dan Kayes was tall and muscled—not so much as Chase—but the two men were obviously friends. Dan had a massive amount of curly blond hair that matched his curly beard.

"What can I do for you, Sir Knight?" Dan laughed. "Wait. You've got a princess on one arm and a lady squire on the other. I'd say you're pretty much set. You don't need me."

His laugh was uproarious and a little snorty.

"You got that right," Chase agreed. "Of course it all depends on the day. Sometimes I need some space, you know what I mean?"

"I know." Dan snorted again. "Are you looking for something fun for the ladies to wear or to tear off you?"

"We're looking for information about the fairy that was killed in the fountain." I felt like I either had to step in or we'd be there the rest of the day listening to Dan laugh about Chase's love life.

Dan sobered at once. "Yeah. That was a bad thing. Have you talked to Merlin? I saw him out there right before everyone started screaming. Maybe he knows something."

Chase looked at me—not Isabelle. "That's the second mention of his name. What do you think, squire?"

Chapter Ten

I opened the door to the clothing shop. "I think we should go to the apothecary and see what Merlin has to say."

There was a shaved ice vendor with dozens of tiny bottles of colored syrups as we crossed the King's Highway near *Sarah's Scarves*. I was suspicious right away when Isabelle sent Chase to get her a raspberry ice and said that we would wait for him.

I waited for him to move out of earshot and got ready for Isabelle's attack.

"You shouldn't be here," she hissed at me. "Leave now and there won't be any hard feelings."

"That's backwards. You shouldn't be here. Maybe if you leave now, Chase won't break up with you until tomorrow."

"You little witch!" Isabelle's petite hands formed claws as she glared at me. "I knew you wanted him."

Of course her rage was a little unimpressive since she

was barely tall enough to see my face without getting on a stepladder. If I'd hit her, I would probably have killed her.

"I don't care if you know. Chase and I were meant to be together. He won't be with you much longer. If I were you, I'd go find another knight to hang on to."

Back in my Village, when Chase was actually with Isabelle, I would never have said anything like that to her. I was completely surprised when he dumped her for me. I mean, look at her. She seemed to be every man's dream. I always felt like a clumsy giantess around her.

But that was then. This was now.

"Chase will always choose me over you." She smiled smugly. "Go have a look in the mirror. You can't compete with me."

"Lucky for me, Chase isn't impressed by all those gilded edges. You being a princess doesn't mean anything to him. Pack it up. He won't be in the castle with you for long."

"He lives in the castle. Where else would he be?"

"He's going to live in the Dungeon when he becomes Bailiff." I hadn't meant to go that far with it. She'd goaded me into it.

We both saw Chase coming back with three ices. I was finished talking to Isabelle anyway, and ready to question Merlin. He probably had nothing to do with the fairy's murder, but this was a different place. Maybe Merlin was different too.

Just as Chase reached us, Isabelle sighed and dropped to the ground in an elegant movement that made her silk dress flow out around her.

Chase handed me the ices and knelt beside her. "Isabelle? Are you okay?"

She put her hand on his arm. "It's so hot. I'm just feeling a little faint. Could you carry me back to the castle?"

"Of course." He glanced up at me. "Go talk to Merlin and let me know what he says. I'll meet you at the dressing room after I take Isabelle to her chambers. Thanks, Jessie."

So there I was with three raspberry ices and Chase

gallantly carrying Isabelle toward the castle. She smiled at me as she put her arms around his neck.

"Well she's annoying, isn't she?" Starshine appeared.

"I'll say. Things were going so well with me and Chase." I handed her a raspberry ice. It was too heavy for her. She had to dump part of it out until it was light enough for her to carry. "I think I might've tipped my hand a little too soon."

"You think so? You mean boasting to the princess that you plan to take her man away?"

"Yeah. I guess so."

"Loose lips and all. Where are you headed now?"

"To see Merlin, the Village wizard. Do you know him?"

She had a pink mustache from the raspberry ice. "Not all magic users know one another, dear. I haven't met him."

I smiled and handed her a napkin. "Sorry. Besides I don't think Merlin has any real magic. He's really just the crazy, corporate type."

As far as I could tell, not one person had noticed the small fairy next to me as I walked between *Galileo's Podium* and across the cobblestones past the *Merry Mynstrel's Stage* to *Merlin's Apothecary*.

Merlin was sitting on a bench outside his shop full of stuffed birds, colored powders, and liquids. And of course, Horace, the disgusting, molting moose head at the door. I handed him the drippy third raspberry ice. He took it from me with a smile.

"I'd like to ask you a few questions about the evening the fairy was killed." I sat beside him.

"For a free ice, you get a free question."

"A few people noticed that you were around the Good Luck Fountain right before the fairy was killed. Did you see anything?"

"I don't recall." His purple starred robe blew around in the light breeze showing his bare legs.

I looked away quickly before I saw anything else beneath his robe. He had a bad habit of flashing women as he went by.

"You don't recall being there or you don't recall seeing the fairy?"

He stared at me with his piercing gray eyes. "I don't recall you being the Village Bailiff, young woman. Have you been appointed without my knowledge?"

"No." I glanced away to watch two men fighting with swords on the cobblestones. "I'm just helping."

"I recently spoke to Detective Almond and your ex-boyfriend who does indeed happen to be the Bailiff. I don't think anything has changed since then."

"You said one question for one free ice," I reminded him. "You've already eaten most of the ice. What about an answer to my question?"

"All right. I honor my deals." He adjusted his pointy purple hat on his grizzled head. "I was around the fountain. I saw the fairy in question. I didn't see anyone kill her, or I probably would have stopped it. Is that all?"

He was putting me off, as he probably put off Detective Almond and Canyon. But I knew his secret and didn't hesitate to use it.

"You look much different in a business suit," I told him. "I often wonder why you live here when the CEO of Adventure Land could live anywhere."

"What?" His face lost its sly look. "How do you know about that?"

"It's enough that I know," I reminded him. "Now, did you see a tall, older man with long brown hair when the fairy was killed? He was probably dressed in red and black armor."

"You're trying my patience," he ground out.

"And you're making me angry. That poor fairy is dead, and there might be another death if her killer isn't stopped. Have you thought of that? The police could close the Village."

"You don't fool around, do you? Maybe you should be the Bailiff. I get the feeling your ex isn't exactly happy in his work."

I saw this as my opportunity to pitch Chase as Bailiff. I could tell Merlin was surprised at the idea, but he heard me out anyway.

"How does the queen's favorite feel about becoming the next Bailiff?" he wondered.

"I don't know. He'd be good at it, and he has better qualifications than Canyon. Not to mention that people tend to be more afraid of Chase than of Canyon."

"I'll take it under advisement—but only if Chase is interested."

"Interested in what?" Chase was close enough to hear the last part of our conversation as he walked up behind me. "What are you telling him, Jessie?"

Merlin laughed. "I think she sees you as our new Bailiff, Sir Knight. How dost thou feel about that appointment?"

Chase took my arm. "Excuse me, Sir Wizard. We are late for the joust. We'll take this up at some future time."

"Why don't you finish questioning Merlin?" I suggested as he propelled me down the cobblestones. "I think he might have something important to say."

"I don't want to be Bailiff," Chase said. "I'm happy being a knight. Quit trying to make people think of me as something that I'm not. I'm only doing this so the police can figure out who really killed Apple Blossom without arresting me for it."

"Okay. You just seem like such a natural at it." I smiled to make my words seem more positive.

"I'm not. Lay off, Jessie, or you'll have to find new employment. I hear they're looking for a new pretzel vendor."

I shuddered. Everyone knew the pretzel job was hard. The Village hardly ever had enough pretzel vendors. I wasn't sure if it was because they had to balance twenty pretzels on a stick as they called out to potential buyers or if it was because they had to buy any pretzels they dropped. Either way, I didn't want the job.

"Sorry. I didn't mean to make you do something you don't want to do."

He let go of my arm. "All my life, people have wanted me to be things I didn't want to be. My parents were the worst. Can you see me as a financial mastermind? I'm happy being a knight. Or at least I will be again when people don't think I killed a fairy."

My heart melted when he explained himself to me.

I knew all about his parents and his crazy brother. I knew he was happy at the Village, which made me happy. Besides, my fairy godmother didn't say anything about him being Bailiff. He just had to fall in love with me again and help solve the fairy murder. No point in getting too ambitious.

"No, I can't see you swimming with the Wall Street sharks." My fingers burned to push aside a stray lock of his long hair. "I'm glad you're happy. I'm sure everything will work out if we can find the killer."

We were at the gate for the jousting event. Lord Dunstable nodded to us as we headed toward the dressing room.

"There's just one more thing," Chase said in a calmer voice. "I don't want you to panic, but I promised Isabelle I'd find another squire. She's crazy jealous of you. I've never known anyone as insecure as she is. I'll talk to the personnel director after the joust. I promise you won't have to sell pretzels."

"But the murder..." I argued as we went inside to get him ready for the joust.

He looked at me with a gentle gaze. "I'm sorry. This is the best I can do. Get my breast plate. We have to get moving, or I'll have to forfeit."

That was true. It had happened to a few other knights. Never to Chase, but he'd never been in this situation before.

I helped him dress, and we went out together. He got his horse as I got my standard to advance on the field.

This was a bigger event—the Queen's Joust—which

always had the best attendance. The queen and her huge group of followers would be in the grandstand, and she would offer her favor to Chase since he jousted in her honor. I could hear the crowd chanting his name as they waited for him to appear on the field.

"Ready?" he asked as he came toward me on horseback.

"Ready." How was I ever going to make Chase love me again? This was a bad time to think about it but I couldn't help it when I saw him there, so handsome and sweet.

"Trust me, dear." Starshine was buzzing beside me. "I won't let you down."

Chase's horse started his regal entrance to the field. I moved with him, holding his standard high. The crowd began screaming when they saw him.

"Oh look!" Queen Olivia called out, a tiny microphone attached to her neckline so she could be heard above the roaring crowd. "It is my champion. They never yell so loudly for anyone else. And who can blame them. Welcome, Sir Chase! Your presence always means a good knight!"

People were stomping their feet on the wood bleachers. Women were calling Chase's name. I moved with the standard to his station and prepared for his joust.

"Today, my champion will face the ominous mystery jouster," the queen continued her narrative. "He won't prevail against my champion, but I look forward to seeing him receive the thrashing he deserves."

The crowd agreed with their loud *Huzzahs!* Chase held his sword high as he paraded with around the Field of Honor. And that was when I noticed the mystery jouster.

He was wearing red and black armor and a helm that disguised his identity. I'd never seen that armor on the field before. It felt like a sign—he could be the fairy's killer.

The crowd booed as the mystery knight took his lap around the field. They were supposed to hate him and want the queen's champion to take the day. It seemed that they had been well coached by the cheerleaders in front of each section.

Except that the left section was supposed to cheer for the mystery knight.

I handed Chase his helm as I took his sword and then gave him a lance. He smiled at me before he put down the visor and advanced on his opponent. I watched him approach the knight, wishing I could see under that helm so I knew the identity of the mystery knight.

The knight never spoke, never gave anything away about himself.

They ran at each other twice, neither one able to unseat the other. They seemed well matched. The mystery knight was confident but not reckless. He held his lance in a steady hand, almost as good as Chase.

"My champion seems distracted," Queen Olivia called out above the noise of the crowd between jousts. "Oh wait. Fie on me. I forgot to give Sir Chase my favor. Oh, Chase!" She sang out. "Come, good sir. Receive my fortune upon your joust."

Chase had no choice but to ride to the Queen's side in the grandstand. She kissed a white handkerchief and sent it flying to him with red lipstick on it. Unfortunately, her aim was off and it missed Chase's lance.

It was my job to retrieve it. I ran to get it out of the sand and give it to him.

At the sound of a horse galloping toward us, I looked up to see the mystery knight. He wasn't waiting for the official start of the next joust. His lance was lowered to reach Chase's midsection where he was most vulnerable. I handed Chase the handkerchief and pointed out the impatient knight. He nodded and turned his horse to face his opponent.

What I didn't count on was the rubber battle axe that suddenly appeared in the mystery knight's hand. It was an illegal move during the joust, but sometimes the riders would toss in a trick or two to get the audience's attention.

The battle axe would have bounced off Chase's armor followed by a lot of booing and hissing from the audience. Everyone loved dirty tricks like these even if they were cheering for the favorite. It kept the joust interesting.

As I moved out of the way of the horses and the battle, I realized that the hard rubber axe was at a different trajectory than I had imagined. It was far too low for Chase. It might have hit his horse, but it seemed to be coming toward me.

There was nowhere to hide. I started to drop to the dirt rather than take a sharp blow to the head. Though it wouldn't hurt someone wearing armor, the hard rubber was painful to unprotected skin.

But the battle axe seemed to have a mind of its own. Before I could reach the ground, it struck its target—me.

Chapter Eleven

Lucky for me the axe wasn't real. It wouldn't split my head open. But the rubber was heavy, and it hurt like crazy, stunning me for a moment.

Chase jumped down from his horse, flinging off his helm and gloves. His lance was in the dirt.

"Someone call 911," he yelled as he knelt beside me.

"Goodness me!" The queen continued to narrate what was happening. "It appears the squire has been injured. I do hope the joust will continue."

To make matters worse, our coastal weather kicked in, and it started raining again. I couldn't get up on my own. I wasn't seriously hurt, but I was dazed. I couldn't figure out what was going on.

Starshine was laughing and doing some kind of happy dance as the rain drenched her. Her tiny face was turned toward the sky.

"What are you so happy about?" I asked her. "Did you do that on purpose? You could've killed me."

"Just wait for it," she sang out gleefully. "You're going to love the results."

"She's talking out of her head," Chase said to the medic who was always on standby during jousts. "But we can't leave her here in the rain. I'll take her to my dressing room. Alert the ambulance when it gets here."

"Of course, Sir Knight," the young man replied.

"Take it easy, Jessie." Chase lifted me in his arms and started walking toward his dressing room. "You'll be fine."

"I'm fine now," I told him. "No head injury. No broken bones. No ambulance. Isn't that Village policy for employees?"

"You're not fine, unless you were saying that I did this to you on purpose." He scrutinized my face. "You were talking out of your head."

"Well you said you wanted to get rid of me." I grinned. "But I know you didn't mean this way. I was talking to the Mystery Knight. Who was he anyway?"

"I don't know." He pushed open the door to his dressing room. "But he's sloppy, throwing something like that without any kind of warning."

"I've seen it dozens of times. I think people forget this isn't a real competition."

He put me down on the lumpy, broken sofa and stood back to stare at me. "Are you sure you're okay? You're going to have a black and blue mark on your forehead. That rubber is hard when it hits you with no protection."

I sat up a little too quickly and was immediately dizzy. "Really. I'm fine. It hurts but nothing life threatening."

There was a quick knock at the door before the medic opened it. "The Main Gate says it's too hard to get the ambulance through the crowd. They suggest we bring her down there if we really think it's necessary."

"It's not." I wobbled to my feet, but was able to stand without help. "Tell them to send it back. Thanks."

He glanced at Chase, who nodded after a moment. The medic disappeared to alert the Main Gate and the ambulance.

"All right. If you think you're not hurt," he said to me. "Let's at least find you somewhere comfortable to lie down."

It was extremely odd that Tony came rushing in at that moment. He had a crazy expression on his face as though he'd been slapped in the head with a rubber battle axe instead of me.

"Jessie? Are you okay?"

"I'm fine. Were you watching the joust?" Tony usually doesn't hang out at the Field of Honor. Too much like work for him.

"No." He put his hand to his forehead. "The last thing I remember, I was talking to a pretty girl in a yellow gown by the Lady Fountain. Next thing I knew, I was here. At least that's what it feels like. I think I need to lie down."

"Not here," I discouraged. Maybe my fairy godmother had set this up so Chase and I would have some quiet time together. I wasn't going to mess that up after she had the axe hit me.

"Well I can't go to my place," he blurted. "There was a flood this morning—broken water pipe. I'm not sure where either of us is going to sleep tonight. Have you completely split with the Bailiff? Maybe we could both sleep there."

"No!" Chase said abruptly. "I'm taking Jessie to the castle. You can sleep here tonight, Tony, if you like."

"Thanks." Tony stared at me with a question in his eyes. "Are you and Jessie—?"

"We're not." I wished he'd shut up. "Don't worry about me. Why don't you go find the woman in yellow?"

"Okay. Good plan." He shook Chase's hand. "Thanks for taking care of her."

Chase mumbled something as he shook Tony's hand and then turned to me. "Are you ready?"

"I don't want to go to the castle. I know the joust is off. Let's go back to the scene of the crime and ask more questions. Maybe we can find the killer today. Wouldn't that be nice?"

My voice sounded desperate and strange. My head still hurt, but I didn't want to waste any time in the castle because of it. Chase and I needed to find the killer. I wanted to go back to my Village more than anything. I wanted to sleep in his arms that night, in our bed, in our Dungeon.

"We're not going anywhere but to the castle." He picked me up like I was a rag doll. "At least you're not. Unless you want to go to the hospital, you have to take it easy the rest of the day."

I leaned my head against his broad shoulder. "Whatever. I just want to go home."

"I know. We'll find you somewhere more permanent soon. In the meantime, you need someone to take care of you."

It was a nice thought. I closed my eyes and let him carry me without protesting. I was surprised when he put me on the front of the horse and climbed up behind me. The rain had slacked off as we ambled away from the Field of Honor. Chase's arms were around me. Everything was right in the world.

What I hadn't counted on was the photo-perfect Image we had created for hundreds of visitors. Cameras flashed, and people yelled, "*Huzzah!*" I kept my eyes closed and ignored them, but I knew it was going to be hard for Chase to do the same. It would only take a few minutes for our pictures to be on the internet.

It created a spectacle. Visitors to the Village loved a romance even more than a fight. They lined up to watch Chase and me ride slowly down the cobblestones. People threw confetti and flowers. It wouldn't have surprised me if Adventure Land began ordering a couple to do this every day.

Chase rode right up to the castle gate. It was still guarded by Gus Fletcher, the huge, ex-wrestler.

"Hail, Sir Knight!" Gus shouted at Chase. "Looks like you've been hunting."

"Get the door, huh, Gus? I'm taking her inside for the rest of the day."

"In a very public way, too. I admire your stamina, sir." Gus saluted him before he opened the door to the castle.

And immediately inside the door stood Isabelle. She was so angry that I thought she might explode.

"What is the meaning of this?" she demanded. "Why are you bringing her here?"

"Because she has nowhere else to go right now. She can have my room until tomorrow."

I was between Chase and Isabelle with them talking across me like I was invisible. It was an odd feeling. I wanted to volunteer to leave and get Chase out of this, but a bigger part of me hoped this was the last straw for their relationship. The sooner they broke up, the sooner I could step in and console my husband.

"You forget that you and I share a room." Isabelle sharply nodded toward me. "She's not sleeping in my room."

"And you forget that I have a room of my own here," he replied. "That's where I plan to take her."

He walked by her—it had to be tiring carrying me around.

"You'll need that room for yourself," she shouted after him. "You're not sleeping in my bed tonight, Chase Manhattan!"

I realized as I peeked over Chase's shoulder that dozens of people had followed us to the castle. They were murmuring to each other and taking pictures. It wasn't the best publicity, but Adventure Land had a policy that any publicity was better than none.

Gus was laughing as he closed the castle door. I shut my eyes again and sighed.

Isabelle didn't follow us to Chase's rooms as I thought she might. He took me to one of the suites used for special visitors to the Village. They weren't rented and could only be gifted by one of the high-ranking employees of Adventure Land or through an invitation by the king and queen.

"You know I didn't mean to cause trouble for you." I sat up as soon as Chase put me on the bed. "I'm okay. Let's go look for the killer."

He gently pushed me back on the huge pile of pillows. "Don't worry about it. Isabelle will get over it. You stay here and rest. I'll let housekeeping know that you're here for the day. Let them know if you need anything."

"Chase—"

"If you don't rest, I'm personally taking you to the hospital and you can't squire for me ever again."

"You already said you have to fire me."

He glanced at the door to the suite. "Yeah, well maybe that's not gonna happen now. This might be it for me and Isabelle."

"I'm sorry. Are you going to take me to the hospital on your horse?"

"No wonder Canyon decided to break up with you," he growled. "You can be really annoying."

"I've been told. But thanks for this. I promise to stay here in luxury and air conditioning all day and let people wait on me. No problem."

"I'll be back later to check on you. No parties or male guests. This is my bed after all."

He leaned over and carefully kissed my forehead.

I was in heaven as he left me. I sighed and enjoyed my expensive surroundings.

"It's worked out for the best, as I said." Starshine was on the bed beside me. "I knew you thought I was crazy, but here you are, in Chase's bed for the night."

"Not exactly what I had in mind but better than sleeping at Tony's place. Thanks for hitting me in the head with the rubber axe."

She giggled. "Oh, any time, dear. What are fairy godmothers for if not to grant your most important wishes?"

I got up and wandered through the suite that was made up of the huge bedroom, a sitting room, and a luxurious bathroom. My clothes were filthy. I stripped them off and decided to take advantage of the enormous marble bathtub before I did anything else. Who knew when I'd have another chance for a real bath?

Housekeeping said they would call *Stylish Frocks* and have a new costume sent over for me. I also asked for a hot fudge banana split to be delivered in about two hours. It seemed like that would be enough time for me to soak off all the dirt and sand.

Starshine flitted around the suite, turning the television on and off, and looking at herself in the mirrored wall by the bed. Her response to her surroundings would have been something I expected from a child. She even hopped up and down on the bed a few times. At least she was enjoying herself.

In the meantime, my bath was full and scented with jasmine bath salts I'd found near the tub. I gladly removed my squire's costume and sank into it with a sigh. The hot water made parts of me hurt that I didn't know were injured. It had been a couple of hard days compared to my soft existence at the *Art and Craft Museum*. I had been a much younger version of myself when I'd worked at the *Field of Honor* in my Village. I knew what needed to be done, but my body didn't like doing it.

I looked in a gilded hand mirror I'd taken from the pink marble cabinet top. My face and the side of my head were already bruised. My hair was full of sand. I slowly sank beneath the water until my whole head was submerged.

I wanted to stay like that longer than I could breathe underwater, but was careful not to make that a wish. I never knew which wishes my fairy godmother was going to grant. I didn't want to end up with gills or something.

There was a strange sound outside the bathtub. It was almost like the air pump on an aquarium. I shot up out of the water and was face-to-face with Chase.

"Sorry." He quickly turned away.

I grabbed the only thing I could find close at hand—the mirror—and held it across my chest. The bubbles that had been there were rapidly fading.

"What's wrong? Did you find the killer already?"

"No. I didn't even make it out of the castle. Queen Olivia and King Harold are holding a special audience to decide about the two duels. I had to come back for you because you're the only witness to both of them."

"Oh."

"They already left something for you to wear. You've got a few minutes to get washed up and dressed before we have to talk to them." He ran his eyes down my naked body.

I sighed and remembered how much I liked it when he looked at me that way.

Chapter Twelve

"Okay." I blinked the jasmine bubbles out of my eyes. "I can be ready. No problem."

I waited for him to leave the bathroom. He didn't.

My heart did a quick leap. He found me attractive enough to ogle even in this Village. There was hope for us.

I did something I would never have done before Chase and I were a couple. I pretended that I didn't know he was looking and slowly got out of the tub, bubbles and all. I thought his beautiful brown eyes would bug out. It was very gratifying since I felt the same way each time I helped him get ready for the joust.

He mumbled something and quickly left the room. I giggled.

"That's the spirit," Starshine said. "Show him what he's missing. You're actually much better looking than Isabelle—in a healthier way."

"I know I'm not a size zero, if that's what you mean." I grabbed a large towel from a heated rack and dried off. "I can handle it. I'd look like a freakish skeleton if I weighed what she does. Besides, if I was as skinny as her, my feet would really look big."

Chase rapped on the door, but didn't peek again. "Who are you talking to? Are you sure you're okay?"

"I'm fine. I'll be out in a minute."

My fairy godmother and I both giggled and then shushed each other. I began to think she was rubbing off on me.

My naked pose against the doorframe between the bathroom and the bedroom was wasted since he was in the sitting room. I sighed as I saw the lovely violet-colored gown spread out on the bed. I thought Portia would send another pair of britches for me. Normally I wouldn't have cared, but it was possible that Chase and I could have dinner together if Isabelle was true to her word and didn't want to see him. The gown would be perfect.

I put it on over the clean violet shift that had come with it. It had a deeper neckline than a peasant would wear unless she was trying to attract attention. I left the corset on the bed. I hated those things. The back of the gown had dozens of tiny buttons. I knew I couldn't reach them. That's why women who could afford such things during the Renaissance could also afford a lady's maid.

That didn't stop me. I walked into the sitting room with the back open to my waist and turned for Chase to button it. We did this at the Dungeon all the time. This was no different in my mind. I hoped it jogged something in him.

"This dress is perfect with your eyes." He applied his fingers to the buttons. "Sometimes Portia can really do the right thing. I bet if Canyon saw you in this, he'd be sorry you broke up."

Canyon? Was he really thinking about him as he buttoned my dress? That wouldn't do.

I slowly pressed myself against him. "Sorry. I kind of lost my balance."

He put his hands on my waist to steady me. "That's okay. I hope you don't have a head injury."

"I don't." I smoothed my hand down the front of my gown as he finished. "I'm fine. How do I look?"

Chase smiled as he took my hand and gallantly kissed it. There was nothing slobbery or too personal about it—he didn't turn it to kiss the palm as he usually did. But it was still very nice.

"You look beautiful. Are you ready?"

I nodded and stepped into the slippers that went with the gown. I tucked my hand into the crook of Chase's left arm, and we went to see the king and queen.

The personal quarters of King Harold and Queen Olivia were more elaborate and more expensive than anyplace else in the castle. They had beautiful tapestries on the wall from all over the world, expensive Renaissance paintings, and sumptuous furniture.

The furniture was heavy, Renaissance inspired, and exactly right for the large rooms. The carpets were woven in shades of red and brown and carefully laid across the stone floor. Heavy drapes hung over the windows that overlooked Mirror Lake. On sunny days, the light streamed in, creating shadows and pockets of color around the room.

I knew it well—I'd cleaned it often when I'd worked here.

King Harold was seated in his favorite chair that had large, carved wood arms. He was a little round, but he was every inch a king. Queen Olivia, despite her enormous appetite for men, maintained her slender figure. Her crown was the same size as the king's. She wouldn't have it any other way.

Livy and Harry, as they were known in the Village, had been the two top sales people for Adventure Land in their day. They'd been offered this sweet lifestyle for their years of service and lived up to their titles whenever possible.

"Your Majesties." Chase bowed and addressed them.

"Sir Knight." King Harold inclined his head, almost

losing his crown. "Welcome."

"Chase!" Queen Olivia giggled almost as much as my fairy godmother. "We are so pleased to see you. We certainly hope your squire is well."

"She is indeed well, Your Majesty," Chase said. "May I introduce Lady Jessie Morton?"

"Oh!" She seemed surprised. "We did not know your squire was a lady."

"Welcome, Lady Jessie." The king laughed. "I daresay the men on the field had no problem discerning which gender you are."

I curtsied. I'm very good at the curtsy, having had years to perfect it.

"Thank you for your kind wishes, Queen Olivia—King Harold. How is Princess Pea?"

The king and queen exchanged puzzled glances.

"Is there a princess in this castle with that name?" King Harold asked.

I realized that Harry and Livy hadn't had a baby yet in this Village. I should have kept my mouth shut or at least not opened it so wide.

"We do not recall any princess by that name." Queen Olivia glared at me as though she'd realized the mistake I'd made.

"Forgive Lady Jessie," Chase said. "She suffers from trauma to the head due to her accident this afternoon."

"Of course." King Harry was quick to understand. "But let us speak about these coming duels, Sir Knight. It isn't that we don't approve a few duels. They are, after all, good for business. The visitors love them. But they must be properly advertised, which is why they must be brought to us for approval."

"We hear that one of the duels is over your lady love, Chase." Queen Olivia fluttered her lashes at him. "Perhaps that is the best reason to duel. It is certainly the one most likely to be understood by the crowd. Did someone say something against Princess Isabelle's honor? You aren't a man to challenge another lightly."

"It was not over love, Your Majesty," Chase said. "The Bailiff laid hands on my squire, Lady Jessie. He was overly familiar with her, and I took umbrage at that since she is my servant."

Again, the king and queen exchanged what those of us in the Village called their 'speaking' looks.

"I don't want you to take this the wrong way, my boy," King Harry said. "But isn't Isabelle a bit put out by your duel over the lovely Lady Jessie?"

"We have not spoken of it, sire," Chase replied. "Princess Isabelle and I are experiencing… other difficulties."

The queen frowned. "And we were so anticipating a royal wedding soon. There's nothing like a big wedding to bring in the crowds."

"By your leave, Majesties," Chase added. "There has never been talk of marriage between myself and Princess Isabelle."

Both the royal personages looked disappointed but carried on with their decision-making process.

"And your other duel," King Harry said. "This is a challenge from Sir Reginald, is that correct?"

"Yes, Your Majesty. He felt that I had dishonored him by leaving the joust before it was finished. I only did so because my squire was injured."

"It seems to me that Lady Jessie might not be your best choice for a squire," Livy drawled.

"Perhaps not, Your Majesty," Chase acknowledged. "But she is my squire and attending to her needs was in no way dishonorable."

Both the king and queen agreed with that.

"We have made a decision," King Harold said. "The duel between you and Sir Reginald shall not commence. Our visitors wouldn't understand honor on the field, I fear."

"But a matter of the heart is quite another thing," the queen said.

"Not a matter of the heart," Chase corrected.

"Yes, yes, I know. But what do you think the crowd will see with the beautiful Lady Jessie standing at your side as you defend her from the bullying Bailiff? I see wonderful internet headlines."

"We need at least a week to get word out to all the news sources and properly advertise the event." The king gestured, and his steward, a dwarf named Marcus Fleck, came forward. "Take care of this, Fleck."

He nodded, and Chase and I were dismissed from the king and queen's chamber.

"Sir Reginald isn't going to like that," I said.

"Neither is Isabelle," he replied.

The rain continued drumming on the roof of the castle. From the windows, I could see the drenched and empty Village far below. I wanted to ask Chase if he'd eat dinner with me. But though I'd been bold in the bathroom, the words wouldn't come. I figured he'd probably take the time to make up with Isabelle.

He walked me back to his room, and we stood outside the door for a few minutes, not saying anything.

"I hope you have somewhere to spend the night," I finally said. "If not, I'm sure you can find some room here. It's a big suite. I could sleep on the sofa."

"Don't worry about it. I'll find a spot in the castle." He smiled. "Just get some rest. Tomorrow we find the killer."

I hoped he was right. I was way past ready to go home.

"All right. Well, thanks again for your help. And your room. I'll see you later."

"Okay."

I opened the door to go inside, my heart feeling like lead in my chest.

"Jessie?" He paused.

"Yes?"

"How about dinner tonight?" He glanced at his watch, the one he wasn't allowed to wear when the Village was open. "In about two hours?"

"That would be great. Thanks."

"See you later."

I closed the door behind me after he'd walked away. Starshine was already bouncing on the big bed. I kicked off my shoes and joined her.

"Dinner with Chase!" she yelled. "That's a great start. Wasn't it at a dinner here at the castle when you knew you loved him?"

"Yes. I was working in the kitchen and dropped one of the big trays that are used to serve food at the King's Feast. Chase stopped to help me clean it up. I knew then that I wanted him to be more than just a friend. He said later that he knew too. Too bad this is only Wednesday. Maybe we could recreate that moment at the King's Feast on Sunday."

"What a wonderful idea!"

"No." I changed my mind. "Bad idea. This has to be over before then. I don't want to live this way until Sunday."

She sighed and stopped bouncing. "All right. We'll see what we can do."

I stopped bouncing, too, and got off the bed.

"You look very nice in that gown. It is a perfect color for you," she observed. "But what about your hair? Maybe you should do something different with it, something exciting."

We went into the bathroom and looked in the big mirror. Starshine stood on the pink marble counter and peered at my reflection.

"What about blond hair?"

My short brown hair was suddenly luxurious blond tresses.

"I look like Rapunzel. I don't have the coloring to be blond.

"All right. What about black as the raven's wing?"

The long blond hair was suddenly black and shiny.

"Too much like Isabelle," I complained. "I think Chase likes my hair the way it is."

"But anything can be improved on, my dear."

My hair went back to being short and brown, but now

there was a lovely crown of violets on it.

"I like that. Thanks."

"What else could we alter that would appeal to your young knight?"

I suddenly felt much heavier and looked down to see that I had become very well endowed—almost to the point of being Dolly Parton.

"I don't think so. How do women even walk with those things?"

She laughed at me. "Men adore them."

"Not Chase." I considered how he'd reacted when I'd worn a corset once before. "Okay. He's not immune. But I'm not going to dinner with him tonight wearing these. What would he think when I didn't have them this afternoon?"

"It's my experience that most men don't think when they see those." She giggled. "But it is your choice."

"Then no thanks. I think he likes the way I look right now. He was getting an eyeful when I got out of the tub."

"That's true."

The extra-large accessories were gone. I smoothed my dress down, glad they weren't really mine.

"I guess you'll do just as you are." She smiled and flitted around me. "You look lovely. I hope you touch his heart."

"Then all we have to do is find out who killed Apple Blossom." I sighed and sat on the sofa in the sitting room. "Do you have any tricks up your sleeve for that?"

"I wish I did, but the killer is unclear to me. Poor Apple Blossom. She was such a dear. I can't imagine who might want to hurt her."

"Don't worry. We'll figure it out."

I stayed in the sitting room and watched a terrible movie on TV. I thought nervously of what I could say or do to make him fall for me. I was glad that I didn't have to put so much thought and effort into wooing Chase in the first place, or we might never have been together.

It was finally time for dinner. A knock on the door heralded a kitchen wench who led me to a covered terrace that overlooked the Village. Chase was there in his best blue velvet doublet that was embroidered with silver. He took my hand and seated me at the small table sheltered from the rain yet still outside in the warm summer evening.

"As I said before, you look amazing in that dress."

"As do you, Sir Knight, in blue velvet."

"I hope you like my choices for dinner."

"I'm sure I will." Absolute truth since I would've enjoyed wood shavings if I was eating with him.

A young harpist played quietly in the corner as Chase dismissed the kitchen wench and served the meal himself. The sun was setting behind the rain clouds that still lingered off the coast, creating a hazy pink glow in the sky. It was a perfect romantic evening. And it made me wonder why he'd gone through so much trouble to impress me.

Was he already on my wavelength? My heart beat double time.

My conversation had to be subtle and seductive. Maybe I'd get a chance to casually touch his hand. But neither one of those options were meant to be.

The door to the terrace burst open. The harpist screamed. A man in red and black armor stood in the doorway with his sword at the ready—the mystery knight—and maybe Apple Blossom's killer.

"Chase Manhattan." A thick, dark voice threatened. "Prepare to meet your doom."

Chapter Thirteen

Chase jumped to his feet as the red knight pushed over the table that held our dinner.

I was a little slower getting out of the way and ended up with wine on my beautiful dress. If Chase didn't smack him, I was going to.

The intruder put his arm around my waist and brought me up against his armor.

"What? No. This isn't happening," I told him. "Get out of here. Leave us alone."

He pushed back his helm—it was Canyon. "Jessie? Don't you recognize me? I've come to fight for you, my lady. I'm not letting this two-bit knight take you away. You're mine."

I heard giggling. My fairy godmother thought this was somehow funny. I didn't think it was funny at all. Of all the things I wanted, Canyon deciding to battle Chase for me wasn't it.

"Let me go." I pushed away from him, noticing as I did that there were scratches and dents in his armor. I'd never seen Canyon wear armor, at least not that I could remember. *But this is a different place. Anything is possible.*

I thought about Apple Blossom. Canyon was a tall, strong man too. He could have been the one who killed her.

"Come on, Chase." Canyon goaded him. "Let's do this so I can take my lady back to the Dungeon."

"Sorry," Chase said. "But I don't think any woman would be impressed that you live in the Dungeon."

He was wrong about that, but I didn't say so. How could he know? He wasn't the Bailiff.

"This area isn't big enough for us to fight." Canyon continued on his course to self-destruction. "I'm afraid I might kick your scrawny butt right off the terrace."

That was it for Chase. He smiled and gestured toward the open hall behind them. "I'm right behind you."

By this time what few members of the castle staff that hadn't heard the ruckus on the terrace had been alerted by the young harpist who'd run out. They were gathered in the big hall that separated the royal chambers from those that were inhabited by visitors. Isabelle was there in a very sheer pink gown. Gus Fletcher was there too. He'd be on Chase's side.

"Here now!" Sir Reginald demanded to know what was going on. "What are you two knaves fighting about?"

"I want my lady back," Canyon bellowed, waving his broad sword around. "I challenge Chase Manhattan to a duel right here, right now."

"You've got it." Chase took his sword out of the scabbard at his waist. "Have at it, Bailiff."

"Chase!" Isabelle tried to get his attention. "You aren't really fighting for Jessie, are you?"

"Stay out of the way," he barked at her, caught up in the moment.

She walked off in a huff but not too far. No doubt she wanted to watch what was going to happen too.

"We do not fight in the castle, young men," Sir Reginald said. "Make an appointment with the king and queen if you want to duel."

But Olivia and Harold were in the crowded hall too.

"That's quite all right, Sir Reginald," Harry said. "Only reruns on TV tonight. The queen and I were bored. Have at it!"

Sir Reginald was almost beyond words. "Your Majesty? You would condone dueling in the castle hall as if it were some low tavern?"

"Quiet, Reginald," Livy said. "Let the two men work this out. I love a duel of passions."

The crowd backed further away from Chase and Canyon, but everyone stayed to watch. Sir Reginald stayed too, but with a sour expression on his sallow face.

"That's it," Canyon said. "Let's do this."

"And to the victor goes the Lady Jessie's heart." King Harold toasted me with his large beer stein. "*Huzzah!*"

The two men started fighting, their blades clashing and echoing in the hall.

No way was I going home with Canyon even if he won the battle—which seemed doubtful to me. I wasn't chattel and couldn't be won with a duel. I was staying with Chase unless someone pried me away from him.

They fought up and down the hall, across the colorful rugs and in front of good copies of historic works of art. Chase lost his footing on the tile once but regained it before Canyon could finish him. Canyon dropped his sword, but Chase stepped back and allowed him to regain it.

"The two are well-matched," a visitor said from behind me. "I'll wager on the one in red armor."

A female voice disagreed. "My money is on the other man. He's gorgeous."

I didn't look behind me, hoping the duel would be over soon. I watched Canyon. He was good on his feet, and his reach was almost as long as Chase's. But it was easy to see that Chase had more experience with a sword.

The dents and scratches on the armor that Canyon wore bothered me. I didn't like the idea that someone I'd chosen to hire for the Village could have murdered Apple Blossom. Maybe this wasn't the same place, but it could also mean that the fairy murdered in my Village had also been killed by him.

Of course a few dents and scratches didn't mean Canyon was the killer either. It was a costly indulgence for men who had full armor. Most of them took good care of it, but knowing the condition of his apartment in the Dungeon, I would have said he wasn't careful with anything. Chase's place, when he'd lived alone, had never looked that way.

Canyon threw his helm to the side. He was sweating in the full armor that also impeded his movements. In comparison, Chase was fast to recover from the thrust and parry of the swords.

The event ended when Canyon lost his balance and fell, face first on the floor. The weight of his armor kept him from being able to flip over and get at Chase. Chase kicked Canyon's sword out of the way and declared his victory with his boot in the middle of the other man's back.

Members of the court, visitors, and staff politely applauded. There were a few *Huzzahs!* followed by a couple of fist bumps. Then everyone began to drift away, back to doing whatever they'd been doing.

To my surprise, Sir Reginald remained with his thin lips pursed and his proud head held high. I understood why a moment later when Gus pushed open the big door to the inner sanctum of the castle—with Detective Almond and two officers behind him.

"The Bailiff?" Detective Almond's voice echoed in the big hall.

"Yes, Detective," Sir Reginald said. "This is the man you're looking for."

Canyon was confused. "Is it illegal now for a man to try to win back his girlfriend? Shouldn't there be some kind of Village justice for that instead of calling the police? I don't even know this place anymore."

He stared at me like a wounded animal, and I felt guilty. I stepped forward and asked what was going on.

"We're detaining the Bailiff," Detective Almond said. "This place is so weird. I guess you don't even remember what that means."

"I think she meant why are you taking him in," Chase clarified.

"Simple. We're questioning Mr. Britt for the murder of Apple Blossom the fairy." Detective Almond rolled his eyes. "Only here would I have to say that."

The two officers took Canyon's armor and sword for evidence. They led him toward the castle gate.

He screamed my name. "I love you, Jessie. I know I've never said it before, but it's true. You have to wait for me. I'll be out of prison in twenty years or so. We can be together then."

The guilt weighed on me even more. I wanted to yell back that he didn't even know me. He couldn't be in love with me. And I wasn't supposed to be with him. It was stupid for him to think that he loved me.

"Are you okay?" Chase asked me.

"I'm fine." I wrapped my arms across my chest. "I don't know what he's talking about. We've never talked about being in love or having a relationship."

"A man says desperate things when he knows his time has come." Sir Reginald rendered his cryptic opinion of the situation before he turned his back and started to his chamber.

"You brought them here," I accused him. "Why did you call the police?"

"The good detective asked me to keep an eye out for red and black armor that had been ill-used," he called back. "I'd say the Bailiff's armor qualified, wouldn't you?"

"Do you really think he killed the fairy?" Chase asked him.

"I neither know nor care," he responded in a flat voice. "Good night to you, sir."

"He gets me." Chase steamed when we were alone. "I'm not a fan of Canyon's either, but Sir Reginald has his regal head up his butt!"

"Detective Almond didn't arrest him just because Sir Reginald called," I reminded him. "It wasn't just the armor either. Canyon fits the description, like you did."

"I saw the marks on his armor," he admitted. "Maybe he had something to do with the murder. I don't know."

"Talk about a mood dampener." I laughed trying to break the tension. "I'm sorry your beautiful dinner was spoiled."

"Yeah. Me too." He nodded toward me. "Your pretty dress too."

We needed to be diverted from what happened. "I guess we'll have to raid the kitchen."

"Can you do that?"

"You've never raided the kitchen, and you live in the castle?" I took his hand. "Trust me. Everyone who lives here raids the kitchen at one time or another. Let's go."

It wasn't the romantic dinner I'd been hoping for, but at least we were together—with five other people raiding the huge commercial kitchen.

One of the queen's ladies-in-waiting was chomping on a pork chop held delicately in a cloth napkin. She was speaking with a squire I didn't recognize.

"I knew it as soon as I saw that armor," she said. "I read the newspaper. It said the fairy kicked at a big man wearing armor. That's why it was so beaten up."

"He didn't even think about cleaning it and taking out the dings before the challenge. It looked a great deal like the suit of armor I threw away for my master yesterday." The squire shook his head. "He would never have worn it for a duel. The oaf probably found it in the trash."

Chase and I grabbed some snacks from one of the refrigerators. There were several Cornish hens and some apples. He put a whole small hen on his plate. I took an apple and some cheese.

We sat outside the kitchen in the dimly lit hall. A throng of people who'd been there for the duel must have suddenly realized that they were hungry. Everyone was talking about the duel and Canyon's arrest between gulps of soda and ale, not to mention mouthfuls of elaborate dessert leftovers and pizza slices.

A few of the knights congratulated Chase on his win.

"But with the Bailiff gone," one man said. "Who will take care of the Village? The police only come out for the big stuff."

"They'll find somebody." His friend punched him in the arm. "Let us away forsooth with worry by quaffing large swigs of ale!"

They laughed and disappeared into the crowded kitchen.

"That's a good question," I said when I had the opportunity. "The Bailiff takes care of so many things that happen every day. They're going to need someone right away."

Chase shrugged, not getting the hint. "I imagine Roger will take over again. Canyon hasn't been Bailiff that long. Roger will be happy to do it. He didn't want to give it up in the first place."

I knew that was true. I'd kind of hoped Chase would step up before anyone had a chance to talk to Roger. I decided to be blunter. "Why don't you do it?"

"What?" He stared at me like I was crazy. "I don't want to be Bailiff. That's a 24/7 job, Jessie. I don't want that kind of responsibility. We talked about this before."

Sighing, I finished my apple and cheese. Chase got us each a glass of wine. We talked comfortably, as old friends do, about what was happening in the Village—minus the murder. I wasn't ready for the evening to be over when we stood to take our plates back into the kitchen.

Two more hungry castle residents came toward us. I wasn't even sure how it happened. One minute I was standing there holding my plate. The next my plate was on the floor. I was beginning to be aware of how magic felt.

Starshine had arranged this because of what I'd told her had happened in the other Village.

"Allow me." Chase was already getting the plate off the floor.

I understood—she was trying to recreate the moment we'd both thought we'd fallen in love. But it didn't have the same feeling this time. It was forced and disjointed. Maybe it was because I was already in love with Chase. Maybe it was because Chase had refused to be the next Bailiff. He'd already been the Bailiff when that magic moment had occurred before.

Whatever it was, I waited awkwardly until he handed me my plate. We went into the kitchen and dropped off the plates and cups. It was as though we'd become uncomfortable with each other instead of falling in love.

"I'll walk you back to your room," he offered. "I wish things had gone differently tonight."

"Yeah. Who knew you were going to have to duel for your supper?" I laughed, trying to get past this weird place we were in. "Do you think the armor Canyon was wearing belonged to someone that had thrown it away?"

"It's possible. Usually squires know their knight's armor better than the knights themselves."

We'd reached his room that he was letting me have for the night. I didn't have any other tricks up my sleeve. I couldn't think how else to engage his interest. I felt lost and alone.

"Would you like to come in for a nightcap from your minibar?"

He smiled at me. "Thanks anyway. I think I should go have a talk with Isabelle. I'll see you tomorrow."

Chase left. I closed the door to his suite behind me. It seemed as though I'd struck out on both counts. He didn't want to be Bailiff, and he was going to make up with Isabelle. I just needed to go to sleep and hope things would be better tomorrow.

"You probably just need a nice glass of warm, mulled

wine," Starshine suggested. "That will fix you right up for a good night in that beautiful bed."

"Maybe. I know want to call the kitchen for it at this time of night. I always hated when guests did that when I worked here."

"Perhaps you should make that a wish."

"Okay." It seemed stupid, but what the heck? "I wish for some warm, mulled wine."

The words were barely out of my mouth when there was a knock at the door. She giggled as I went to answer it. Magic was definitely in the air.

It was Chase, holding of all things, two mugs of mulled wine.

"I was thinking about it." He smiled. "I'd rather have a drink and talk to you than see Isabelle tonight. Is that invitation still open?"

Chapter Fourteen

Dazed, I blinked.

But I wasn't at the door welcoming the love of my life into his rooms.

Instead, I was in his big, beautiful bed. And Chase was sleeping, naked, beside me.

I jumped up, caught my foot in one of the blankets, and fell on the floor. I was naked too! I tried to make a graceful exit and tripped over my pretty dress from last night.

Oh my gosh!

It was either magic or the worst mulled wine ever. I couldn't remember a thing since seeing Chase with the mugs of wine at the door. I knew it was morning because Carolina sunshine was spilling through the mullioned windows.

"What did you do?" I whispered to my fairy godmother. "You can't just magic these things. A dress, sure. Or a situation, maybe. But not this one. He's going to feel trapped and angry. He'll think I'm as devious and underhanded as Isabelle. This will never work."

"Good morning, Jessie." Chase was smiling as he stared down at me. "What are you doing down there? Come back to bed."

Wait. What?

Maybe it had worked. Maybe it was okay. After all, I loved him in this life and the other one. Maybe he loved me too. I knew Chase never had random flings with women in the Village. I always thought it was because he knew people trusted him as Bailiff. But maybe it was more— an intrinsic part of his personality.

"Good morning." I smiled as tentatively as a new bride on her wedding night. "I-uh-forgot the bed was so high. That first step was a doozy."

I pushed myself to laugh and snorted. That sobered me. I reached for my wrinkled gown, pulling it up against my bare body.

"It's not even eight," he said. "We have plenty of time. Shall we order breakfast in bed?"

After wanting this so badly, it was suddenly moving too fast for me. I ran into the bathroom and closed the door like the hounds of hell were after me.

Now what?

"What are you doing, dear?" Starshine appeared, wrinkles between her tiny brows as she stared at me. "You're going to undo all the good you've done. Get back in there and woo that man."

"I think the wooing is over." I paced the warm tile floor. "I didn't know this would happen. Not like this anyway. What was in that wine?"

She giggled. "Just a sprinkling of pixie dust."

"I thought that made you fly?"

"Pixie dust can help you do whatever is in your heart, Jessie. If it wouldn't have been in Chase's heart to stay with you last night, it wouldn't have happened."

He knocked on the door. "That's a big bathtub. There's

room for two."

Starshine smiled. "I assume you can handle it from here. It's not your first rodeo with this show pony." And she vanished.

"Jessie? Are you okay?" he asked.

She was right, my addled brain told me. This was Chase. My husband, and hopefully someday, the father of my children. I knew him. He knew me. This was absolutely right.

I opened the bathroom door and assumed the pose, leaning against the doorframe with my hand on my hip—the provocative pose he'd missed yesterday.

"I'm fine. Just making sure the water is hot."

* * *

Two hours later, we were dressed and headed into the Village.

We'd had a wonderful breakfast of strawberries and French toast with mounds of powdered sugar. It was even better looking at Chase while I was eating. I'd conquered the part about him wanting to be with me. Now we just had to solve the murder.

I was wearing the men's britches and blousy white shirt again. Portia had even found me a clean pair of boots. The day was before us. Anything was possible.

"Would you like to get coffee before we head over for the joust?" Chase asked with a big smile on his face.

"That sounds great. We can talk about whether or not we think Canyon is actually guilty of murder."

He put his arm around me. "I really don't care. The police are off my back about it. I think we should let them do their job."

I stopped walking to stare at him. This was Chase, right?

"But what about the squire saying the armor might belong to another knight? I have a feeling Detective Almond arrested Canyon because of the armor and his description matching what Blueberry saw. That's not necessarily what happened. We have to finish asking around."

"Jessie." He kissed me and held me tight. "Really. I'm

ready to joust, and I need you to be my squire. Besides, I might get jealous with you spending so much time thinking about your ex."

"Canyon wasn't my ex," I said. "We were only sort of . . . dating. But that doesn't mean I want to leave him in jail if he isn't guilty."

"I'll tell you what—let's hand over all these questions to Roger. I'm sure he's going to take over again as Bailiff. He'll know what to do."

I agreed, and we walked through throngs of visitors entering the Village through the Main Gate. The scantily clad girls from the *King's Tarts* pie shop were giving out more than pie samples, as usual. The minute they saw Chase, they wanted to give him everything.

I intervened and took his arm to lead him around to where Master Archer Simmons was having his troop of archers shoot flaming arrows into the blue sky. The arrows dropped harmlessly into Mirror Lake but made a fantastic show.

Roger Trent lived above his shop, *The Glass Gryphon*. He was an artistic maker of fine glass pieces. He was also a pain in the butt, only mitigated when he'd finally married basket weaver, Mary Shift from *Wicked Weaves* across the cobblestones from him.

I'd apprenticed with both of them and had the scars to prove it.

We found Roger outside his glass shop with a cast on his leg. He was in his fifties, still in good condition, his shaved head as sun-darkened as his face. He was the first Bailiff in the Village, if you didn't count Detective Almond. Roger fit the bill nicely as a retired police officer who'd always had a passion for glass.

"What happened, Roger?" Chase asked when he saw his leg.

"I took a tumble off the climbing rock yesterday. Wouldn't you know the king would ask me to take over as Bailiff again? I can't do anything like this. I'm glad I have a good apprentice. Otherwise I'd have to close the shop too."

"What about Mary?" I asked without thinking.

"Mary Shift?" He glanced across the street. "What about her?"

I realized as he said it that they weren't together. This was something else messed up because of my wish. "Just wondering about her." I shrugged, feeling lame and stupid.

"Anyway." Roger turned back to Chase. "Not sure what we're gonna do about a Bailiff for the next six weeks until I get this cast off. It sounds like Canyon is gone. I wouldn't have pegged him for a killer, even with my experience as a police officer."

"Thanks anyway." I pulled Chase away before we could hear endless repetitive stories of Roger's glory days on the job.

"That's too bad," Chase said. "I don't know anyone else who could do it."

"You mean besides you?"

"Jessie—"

"You're the man for it. You've got experience as a paramedic. You understand the law because you're an attorney. Maybe they'll waive the six weeks' training with the police since this is an emergency. I know Detective Almond doesn't want to be here every day."

"I think we should head for the *Field of Honor.*" He started walking that way.

"You're so much more than a jouster," I encouraged him. "You could do this, and we could find Apple Blossom's real killer."

"What makes you think Canyon didn't kill her?"

"Because I just can't see him that way, can you? He's kind of crazy, but I don't think he'd hurt anyone."

"I don't know. I think he wanted to kill me last night. As for who he really is—I guess you'd be the best judge of that."

A group of knight groupies surrounded us to get Chase's autograph on everything from small swords they'd bought at one of the shops to their arms and dresses. Yes, they were all women.

I stood off to the side, realizing I was never going to talk Chase into becoming Bailiff. His motive for caring who killed Apple Blossom had vanished with Canyon's arrest. I didn't think it was because he didn't care—it was more the attitude of it not being his job.

We continued on to the *Field of Honor* where they were preparing for the first joust of the day. Horses were being exercised and hay spread on the field. Squires were shining their masters' armor and someone was testing the loudspeaker at the grandstand.

I got Chase ready for his joust, but I was thinking the whole time about the murder.

It seemed to me that I had to talk with Canyon and Detective Almond to find out what was really going on. I was pretty sure Canyon hadn't confessed to killing Apple Blossom. But if he wasn't responsible, who was? And who in the Village could take over as Bailiff?

"You're quiet," Chase observed as he pulled on his gauntlets. "Still thinking about Canyon?"

"Only in the sense of wondering if the police have the right man." I kissed him lightly on the lips.

"You have to let them work, Jessie. They'll figure it out."

But I was still mulling it over after the joust as Chase was swallowed by fans, men and women, that showered him with flowers for his winning event.

"Don't think you can keep him for long." Isabelle stepped beside me, and we both watched him. "I know what it's like to want him in your life. There's no one like Chase. He broke up with me last night. I'm sure you know all about it."

"He didn't mention it," I said in what I hoped was a kind way. I didn't want her to think we were talking about her.

She sighed. "It's all over the Village. My lady-in-waiting told me. She knew about it this morning before tea."

"I'm sorry. I know you care about him."

"Just a friendly warning—enjoy him while you can. It won't last long."

I watched her walk away with dozens of male eyes following her. Isabelle wouldn't have a problem finding another lover. She always had someone on a string.

Chase was signing autographs again. While it was part of my job to get him undressed, I was too anxious to wait while his fans had finished adoring him. An idea had come to me that I wanted to explore.

With my determination firmly in place, I strode confidently through the Village where the *Three Chocolatiers* were doffing their large feathered hats to welcome guests into their chocolate shop. Sometimes they did some swordplay outside to mimic their Three Musketeers theme.

Bawdy Betty was out singing her fresh bagels song hoping to bring in some visitors, and the smell of barbecue from the *Three Pigs Restaurant* was wafting down the cobblestones.

I arrived at *Merlin's Apothecary* as a troop of Boy Scouts were admiring his collection of dead animal bones. Merlin was right there with them so he could identify the animals. *Eww.*

"May I have a word with you when you're finished?" I asked with a smile for the scouts.

"Lady Jessie? What may I do for you this day?" He bowed awkwardly and almost lost his pointy hat.

The Boy Scouts laughed and took dozens of pictures. They asked just as many questions about why I wasn't dressed like a girl and how I got so tall.

"Have you ever played a giant in the Village?" one sweet, apple-cheeked little boy asked.

"Yes," I replied. "They had to find me another job because I kept eating Boy Scouts for lunch."

That set them back a piece or two. Merlin frowned and apologized before he turned over the tour to his large-breasted assistant who wore her bodices too tight at his behest.

"What are you trying to do?" He tugged me out of the shop. "Boy Scouts appreciate my collection better than anyone."

"I want to get your attention about an important matter," I said. "We need a new Bailiff since Canyon is in jail."

"What about Chase? Weren't you singing his praises for the job?"

"Yes. But he's not in the job market right now." I took a deep breath. "I want to be the new Bailiff."

He laughed until he could tell by the look on my face that I was serious.

"You're tall enough, I'll grant you that. But I think a large man is in order."

"We don't have time to look for a large man who's interested in the job." I told him about Roger. "We need someone to take over the dead fairy investigation right now."

He stroked his straggly white beard. "I thought the police had arrested Canyon, hence our lack of Bailiff."

"True. But he may not be guilty. You don't want another dead fairy to turn up, do you?"

"No, but Jessie, the king and queen are never going to allow you to be the Bailiff, even temporarily."

"Then you'll have to convince them, won't you?" I smiled. We both knew I had the upper hand.

"Me?" He fluttered his purple robe. "I'm just the Village wizard. Why would they listen to me?"

"You know why. Don't act stupid. Find a way to convince them, or I blab your secret."

He looked shocked. "You wouldn't!"

"I would—unless you convince them to make me Bailiff."

He wiped perspiration from his forehead. "All right. But you better not screw it up. There's one thing you don't know about this place, and I'd hate to be the one who has to show you the inner workings of the Village."

"Are you talking about the old Air Force jails under the

Dungeon?"

"How do you know that?"

I laughed and sauntered away from him. "Just get it done, wizard."

Chapter Fifteen

I convinced Chase that we should check on Canyon at the police station. I figured he actually had legal credentials and could get us inside for a meeting and some information.

He wasn't happy about going but he was very handsome in his black suit and tie. I'd managed to wrangle something a little less Ren Faire-looking from Portia—a long black skirt and a pink top that came close to street wear.

"Are you sure you want to do this?" He was cranky. "It's only two hours until the next joust, and we haven't had lunch."

I straightened his tie. "We have to find out why the police arrested Canyon. I'm sure it wasn't just because of how he looks and his armor."

"All right. But you're buying me lunch someplace nice in the outside world."

"Deal," I agreed, though I had no money. "Let's go."

Chase drove to the police station. I offered to do it but he kind of snarled at that idea. He was still trying to figure out how I'd known where to find his spare key.

At the station, the woman at the front desk recognized both of us. She took one look at Chase's credentials, and walked us back to a small room where she assured us Canyon would be brought to confer with his attorneys.

"If they question me, I'll have to admit I'm a patent attorney," Chase whispered when she was gone.

"Don't worry. It'll be fine."

"How can you be so sure, Jessie? How do you know suddenly so many secrets? Are you psychic?"

"No. Just clever and resourceful."

The door opened, admitting Canyon and a jail guard. Once he was gone, Canyon started blubbering. "You have to get me out of here. Just look at me. I'm wearing an orange jumpsuit. Orange has never been my color."

"Calm down," I advised. "Have you seen a public defender yet?"

"No." He sniffed. "They still haven't actually charged me with anything. I might be in here for years before a trial. I'll be old and none of my clothes will fit."

"You won't be in here for years." Chase read through his files. "They don't really have anything on you. It's all circumstantial. That's why they haven't officially charged you. They're probably hoping you'll break down and confess."

Canyon wiped his nose on his shirt sleeve "I just like living at the Ren Faire and wearing leather. I didn't kill anyone. I like fairies. They're fun and playful. And sexy. Sorry, Jessie."

Chase looked at me. "All I see in here is the armor and the description of the killer."

The door opened again and Detective Almond joined us.

"It's you two, huh? Which one of you is Bailiff now?"

I got to my feet. "The king and queen are appointing me to the post later today."

It was hard to say which man in the room was more surprised.

Detective Almond shrugged. "Okay. Why not?"

With his acceptance of my position came the ability to ask questions. How many of these meetings had I sat through with Chase as Bailiff?

"I think you have the wrong man, Detective," I said. "We know that the armor Canyon was wearing last night wasn't his."

"You do?" Canyon asked.

"Yes. We overheard a squire saying that his master had thrown away a red and black suit of armor yesterday. We think Canyon picked it up in the trash for the duel."

"That's true." Canyon nodded hopefully. "I saw it out there after I had a few beers and decided to put it on to go get Jessie—I mean—the Bailiff."

"I don't suppose you know who it belongs to?" Detective Almond asked. "Because the ME found traces of Apple Blossom's slipper material wedged in the separations between the armor seams."

"No. But we're going to find out by questioning the squire. Does that mean the owner of the armor is the killer?" I asked.

"Unless the fairy was attempting to climb up the outside of the knight's armor," Detective Almond drawled. "That should do it."

"So we can take Canyon back to the Village?"

"No. Not until you find me a better suspect."

"All right." I grabbed the file from Chase. "We'll be back. Or we'll call."

"I'm sure you will." Detective Almond shook my hand, a smile playing on his face. "Good day to you, Lady Bailiff."

Canyon was complaining as they led him out of the room and back to his cell. My heart was pumping as Chase and I headed for the front door. This was going to work. I could feel it. No magic, but a plan was coming together.

"Wow." Chase said as we got outside. "Just wow."

"What? Someone had to do it. It couldn't happen otherwise." I peeked at him while he took out the car keys. "I can handle it."

"When were you going to mention this to me?" he asked. "When did it happen?"

"While your fans were adoring you. I went to see Merlin. He promised to make the king and queen appoint me as Bailiff."

"I don't even know where to start with how wrong this is. Look at Roger—he was a cop for twenty years. He's really tough and wouldn't mind shooting someone if he had to. Look at Canyon he's . . . big. He'd be able to throw himself at a fleeing shoplifter to stop him from leaving the Village. How would you handle something like that?"

"I'm really good with a sword and a bow. I can kick butt when I have to. Don't make me sound like some dainty princess who calls for help when her pinky nail breaks."

He didn't start the car. "I'm sure you could take care of yourself in normal situations with mostly polite men who didn't really want to hurt you."

Was this the way my Chase felt about me too? I didn't think so, but on the other hand, no one had to talk him into being Bailiff after Roger either.

"You can still do it," I assured him. "I'm only doing it because no one else will."

"Is that what this is all about? You're going to shame me into being Bailiff because you're my girlfriend?" His dark eyes weren't happy with that idea.

"No. One way or another, we have to figure out who killed Apple Blossom. You can ignore me, or you can help me. Your choice."

We didn't say anything on the way back to the Village. We didn't even stop for lunch. Chase parked the car, and I got out. Maybe it was too soon for ultimatums. Though our relationship was longstanding for me, it was new to him. I wouldn't have done this when we were first together. I didn't know what to expect.

Chase was a good person, someone who would never look the other way when anyone was in trouble. I knew he didn't like Canyon. I took a chance that he might respond to a challenge from me taking over as Bailiff.

But maybe I was wrong. Maybe this Chase just wanted to joust and live at the castle. Maybe he wasn't the person I was expecting him to be.

I waited for him in the steamy parking lot. He took off his suit coat in the hot summer sun.

"Okay. I'm in." He looked at me and smiled. "If you're the new Bailiff, I must be your right hand man. But you have to promise not to go off on your own and face down the killer. Right?"

"Right." I let out a long sigh of relief and hugged him. He kissed me and we walked toward the employee gate. "Do you want to live in the Dungeon until Canyon is free?"

"That place is a dump. We can still live at the castle. I don't only have a room there because of my relationship with Isabelle."

"No." I laughed. "You have a room there because Queen Olivia lusts after you."

"I have a room there because I pay for it every month. The thing with me and Livy is only in her imagination. I don't mess with other men's wives."

We talked about finding the young squire we'd heard in the kitchen. We both knew it would be easy. There weren't that many squires at the castle. He had to serve someone who lived there.

"You know," he said. "Just because Detective Almond thinks the killer is someone who lives at the Village doesn't mean he's right. Maybe Apple Blossom had a jealous boyfriend who stalked her here."

Now that was the Chase I knew—even though I thought he was wrong. That happened quite a bit. We worked it out, and we would here too.

It was a silent, consensual thing that we were going to share his suite at the castle. I knew that would include angry looks from Isabelle, but I'd endured that before. We walked there together as we talked about the procedural aspects of how we'd work out our new partnership.

"So I help you with the investigation." Chase summed up as he replaced his corporate look with his leather Ren Faire one once we were behind the closed door to his rooms. "And you continue being my squire."

"I'm not sure I can do that and be Bailiff." I replaced my street wear with my britches and blousy shirt. "I'll have to do other things."

"What kind of other things? I've never been Bailiff or paid much attention to what Roger or Canyon did, but it doesn't seem like all that much."

"Help out with runaway camels and people who fall into the fountains. And visitors who get stuck on the top of the climbing wall. And middle of the night emergencies such as the stadium lights not turning on over the Village Green for cleaning, and loose cobblestones being flagged and replaced."

"Really?"

"Yes." I kissed him and smiled. "I know all about being Bailiff."

"From your time with Canyon?"

"Not exactly. But let's just say I know everything a Bailiff does. And I'm afraid I won't be able to continue as your squire. But there are bound to be some loose squires out there somewhere. I'll help you look for one."

Garbed in our Renaissance finery, we hastened to Peter's Pub for lunch. It was just as well that we were too angry to eat in the car on the way back. My credit was good with Peter Greenwalt and his sister who ran the pub, but not so much in the outside world. Chase offered to pay for our lunches. I gallantly told him to put his Lady Visa away.

"You two make such a cute couple." Peter stroked his long brown mutton chops. "Good luck."

Chapter Sixteen

The town crier was out on the King's Highway with the latest news from the Village.

"Oh, unhappy day! Another death at Renaissance Faire Village. Oh terrible day."

"Looks like a job for the Village Bailiff," Chase said. "I still have a few minutes before the joust if you want me to come with you."

"Not really. You're going to have to get your own armor on. Don't worry. This will be very public. I won't be in any danger. You can be my right hand man after the joust."

"*Huzzah!*" He grinned. "Be careful. I'll see you later."

Marcus Fleck was waiting outside Peter's Pub. "The king and queen need a word with you, Lady Jessie."

"What about the murder?"

He shrugged. "It might be good if they officially declared you Bailiff before you begin investigating, don't you think?"

"All right. Has someone summoned the police?"

"The wizard," he said. "He's the one who told me to come get you. This way, my lady."

We walked up the hill to the castle—the second time for me. Gus bowed deeply to me at the castle door, making it almost impossible for him to goose me. I still kept my butt away from him. I knew him too well to trust his randy fingers.

Marcus took me to the same chamber Chase and I had been summoned to for the discussion about Chase's upcoming duels—both of which had now gone awry. He'd lost the advertising for the romantic duel when Canyon had attacked us here.

I bowed respectfully to the king and queen. No curtsies when wearing pants.

"Lady Jessie." The king fingered his beard thoughtfully. "Are you certain you are up for this task?"

"Yes, Your Majesty."

"But you are a woman." Queen Olivia pointed out. "Do you think it wise to take on this role at a time when there is danger in the Village?"

"I can think of no better time, Your Majesty. Even now a new crime calls out for justice. There is no one else to answer it."

The king and queen conferred quietly. They faced me a moment later.

"We are content to allow you to take on this challenge, Lady Jessie." The king's regal tone echoed in the room. "If you encounter any difficulty, please advise us."

"*Huzzah!*" the queen said.

I bowed again. The interview was over. I was officially the new Bailiff of Renaissance Faire Village.

Could this thing get any weirder?

"Congratulations." Starshine beside me as I walked out of the castle.

"Thanks, I guess. I think I missed something along the

way since I couldn't get Chase to do it. Is that going to count against me?"

She giggled—of course.

"It doesn't work that way. You'll know when you've done just the right thing because the wish will reverse and you'll be back in your Village."

"But in the meantime, how am I supposed to know when I'm spinning my wheels? How do I know when I've done something right or when I'm headed in the right direction?"

"Oh, you'll know, dear. You have very good instincts." She sniffed the air. "Is that brownies? Oh, I just love a good brownie, don't you? Not the pesky living ones. I could do without those. I mean the rich chocolate brownies that are slightly gooey in the middle. Excuse me. I'd prefer not to see another dead person if it's all the same to you."

That was fine with me. She wasn't much help in a practical situation. I wasn't really sure she was any help at all.

It wasn't hard to tell where the murder had taken place. A huge crowd of residents surrounded the area that was marked with yellow police tape and barriers. The same tape and barriers were used to block off rides that weren't working or when the elephants were sick.

Detective Almond and Officer Grigg were already there. Because of restrictions on motorized vehicles when the Village was open, the crime scene team was forced to walk in through the Main Gate. An ambulance could come in and drive down the cobblestones but they usually refused if the Village was crowded.

"Good morning," I greeted my new compatriots. "What have we got?"

Officer Grigg snickered. Detective Almond glanced my way and shook his head.

"See for yourself, Lady Bailiff." Officer Grigg stayed where he was.

"Thanks. I will."

It was the young squire from the castle kitchen last

night—the one I'd hoped to talk to.

I wished I'd gone back and talked to him last night. If he had important information it was gone now. It appeared that one of the older castle maids might know something about him. She was sobbing heartily, several other maids attempting to comfort her.

"This is Jordan James, age twenty-two, originally from Topeka. I'm sure there's a story that goes along with that." Detective Almond consulted his notebook. "His mother is Amanda James. That's her right over there. She got him the job at the castle where she's worked for the past five years."

"I know him. He's the one who said his master had him throw away the suit of armor that Canyon said he found in the trash."

Detective Almond raised his brow. I didn't even know he could do that. "That's a little convenient, isn't it? The only possible witness who could save your Bailiff buddy and now he's dead."

"Don't look at me. I didn't kill him. But it's possible someone else told his master that he was shooting his mouth off in the kitchen. We'll have to question everyone in the castle who has a squire."

"I'm glad you're on the job, Lady Bailiff." Detective Almond slapped me on the shoulder. "You're gonna save me a lot of legwork with that attitude. I love a volunteer, don't you, Grigg?"

"Yes, sir." He nodded as though his life depended on it.

There was something almost devilish in having an idea about how things were going to work. I knew what had happened to Grigg in my Village. I knew it wouldn't take much to put him over the edge here.

"This is our second homicide in as many days." I paced the short space around the dead squire as if I were Sherlock Holmes. "The remainder of us in the Village need protection. I suggest you leave one of your officers here in plain clothes to keep an eye on things until the killer is caught."

Detective Almond nodded. "Good idea, Bailiff. Grigg,

you're my best man. If anyone can handle it, you can. The Bailiff will set you up with an identity and get you some crazy clothes. You'll report in at least once a day."

It was easy to see that Grigg wasn't happy with the idea. He didn't argue with his boss, but he looked jumpy.

"Don't worry." I slapped him on the back. "I know just the place for you."

"I'll get back with you when I know the autopsy results," Detective Almond told me. "I think he was strangled like the fairy—one-handed again. Whoever is responsible for this is a powerful man."

"But not Canyon," I suggested. "And if the murders are the same, may I suggest you release him at once?"

"You may suggest it," Detective Almond said. "But until I know the same person killed both people, without a doubt, Mr. Britt stays where he is in my fine jail cell. *Huzzah!*"

"All right." At least I'd tried.

I walked away from the police to follow the castle maids who were urging their friend to leave the scene of her son's death. They had to know who Jordan was working for. It would be easy after that.

Or so I thought.

"Well he wasn't working for any one master," Amanda said tearfully. "He was lucky to find a place here. I thought he could get into a better spot after a while."

"I'm so sorry." If Chase and I hadn't heard Jordan talking in the kitchen, we wouldn't have known about the armor. On the other hand, the young man might still be alive. "Where was he sleeping? I'd like to take a look at his things."

"He was staying in that little storeroom off the kitchen," Amanda said. "He was always a small boy. He didn't need much space, but you're welcome to have a look. I hope you can find out what happened to him."

I hugged her. Not very Bailiff-like I supposed, but I felt so bad for her.

The ladies continued on their way, comforting their

grieving friend.

Grigg caught up with me. "Is that your plan? Are you going to hug everyone to make things better?"

"You run your precinct the way you want to. I'll run my Village the way I want to. Let's go get you some clothes. You kind of stick out here."

He glanced away at the activity in the Village. "I'd rather stick out in this place. I can't believe Detective Almond is going to leave me here undercover."

"You never know. You might like it." I knew he would as soon as he was used to it. Advance knowledge. I wish I had it in my Village too.

"Just kidding," I muttered. "Not really a wish."

"What did you say?"

"Nothing."

We went over to *Stylish Frocks* where there was a long line waiting for costumes. I hated waiting in this line and didn't mind using my new status to cut ahead of everyone. "Look out. Bailiff business. Step aside." The line grudgingly parted for me.

"You know you're not dressed like Canyon Britt," Grigg told me. "You need some leather, right?"

"I don't think there are any costume rules about being Bailiff. And leather here when it's ninety degrees with eighty percent humidity just seems stupid."

He looked me in the eye—we were about the same height. "I guess you can scare the criminals away by threatening to hug them to death."

We couldn't reach the costume window fast enough to suit me. What had happened to the Grigg in this Village? Maybe he wouldn't stay.

"Costume?" Portia asked in a voice that was worse than bored.

"Pirate," I told her. "For him, anyway. I'm fine, thanks."

She handed him a pirate costume complete with tacky hat and red kerchief.

"I don't want to be a pirate," Grigg told me. "Maybe a

knight would be better."

"In the Village, residents don't wear a knight's armor unless they're really knights," Portia informed him. "Jessie, I have something for you."

She handed me a wide leather belt. It was at least eight inches of hot leather that would go around my waist. But even as I thought about complaining, she also handed me a two-way radio. I was in heaven.

I had always coveted Chase's radio. Only a few characters in the Village were allowed to have one. I took the heavy belt and radio with a smile. I didn't want it to last forever, but it was sweet to finally be synced with everything happening around me.

"So where do I change?" Grigg interrupted my private moment.

"Any of the shops will let you change clothes. Just show them your ID card."

"I only have my badge."

"That will work—unless you want to change in a privy. I've done it before. I wouldn't recommend it. Report to the pirate ship over by Lady of the Lake Tavern. That's where it berths. After that, they'll tell you what to do. *Huzzah!* my lord pirate. Good fortune to ye."

He stalked away with a dark scowl. I tried to remember if the Grigg in my Village was as unhappy as this one when he first went undercover. I was pretty sure he was, though maybe not as obnoxious.

Then I walked up to the castle with my utility belt wrapped around my hips rather than my waist. Gus saluted smartly as I walked by. I saw his hand reach to goose me and spun around to confront him.

"If you do that while I'm Bailiff, I will put you in the stocks for a day of Vegetable Justice, sir. Keep your hands to yourself."

Pleased with myself when he backed off, I developed a swagger that would match my new position. As Bailiff, I couldn't sway in a gown anymore. I had to look tough and ready for anything.

As I reached the kitchen, a call came in on the radio. One of the horses that pulled the Cinderella carriages had gone for a joy ride through the Main Gate bearing its terrified coachman and rider with it.

"Lady Bailiff." Sir Reginald made a deep bow to me. "I believe your duty calls."

Chapter Seventeen

Four hours—one crazy horse, three geese who wanted to nest in visitor's hats, and two visitors who removed their clothes and jumped into a fountain later—I was back at the castle.

I knew Chase's job was hard. I knew he was called out of bed, away from meals, and at other inconvenient moments, but I never really appreciated it until that day.

Everyone had a problem they wanted me to resolve. There were children who'd dropped their pretzels on the ground and goats who ate them—the pretzels, not the children. The blacksmith was having a feud with one of the knights and 'accidentally' hit him with the sword he was refusing to accept.

It had only been with the flat side of the sword against the knight's bottom, but it was enough to cause an issue. There was a line of twelve people waiting outside the

Dungeon for Vegetable Justice, which the Bailiff was supposed to preside over as judge and jury.

I told them to come back later. I had no idea where the squishy fruit and vegetables were supposed to come from to throw at them. I thought I knew everything about this job. I was wrong.

But I was back at the castle and hot on the trail of Apple Blossom's killer. I hoped it was the same person who'd killed Jordan the squire. It would be a lot easier that way.

The supply closet was small and packed with a lot of dried beans. With all the meat usually served at the castle, I wondered why they had so many beans.

Jordan's space was in one corner. His mother was right. He didn't have much. There was a sleeping bag and a small pillow. Not many personal items beyond soap, razor, etc. No real feel for the man at all. I shook out his sleeping bag hoping a journal or pictures would fall out. All I got was some dirty socks.

It struck me how brazen both of these crimes had been. They hadn't been committed in the night when they could've gone undetected for hours. Instead both murders had happened out in the open—in broad daylight while the Village was still teeming with visitors. That took some guts.

What kind of person wasn't afraid of getting caught? I could understand why Detective Almond had arrested Canyon. He was big. He was possibly wearing the armor the killer had worn while he got rid of Apple Blossom. And the Bailiff was someone everyone expected to see walking around the Village.

The murders had been brutal, but they had also been accomplished quickly, before anyone had really noticed what was going on. Maybe I had been wrong in championing Canyon's cause. It was possible that he was the killer—at least Apple Blossom's killer.

He and Chase were so different here. How different was the question.

"As different as the moon and the sun." Starshine

appeared to elaborate on the subject. "You've already seen the difference in Chase because he didn't become Bailiff. Everyone here was changed in one way or another by your wish."

"Come on. I'm only a minor character. I can see where Chase is different because my wish affected him personally. I don't see where it could have that much impact on anyone else."

"Is that the only person you've noticed who's changed?"

I thought about her question. "No. Roger and Mary aren't together. Wanda and Isabelle are still alive."

"Exactly."

"Do you know who the killer is?" I narrowed my gaze in what I hoped was an intimidating manner. After all, I was a lot bigger than her. "If you know, you should tell me right away before someone else gets hurt."

She giggled. I could tell she was terrified.

"Even if I knew, I couldn't tell you. That would interfere with your wish. Who knows where you might go from there?"

"How about if I wished that I knew who the killer was?" I tested her resolve.

Her little wings buzzed her right up into my face. "Is that a wish?"

Our eyes locked as though we were having one of those competitions to see who would look away first.

If that was it, I lost. She giggled and disappeared.

I'd read the fairy tales with the fairy godmothers in them. No one ever mentioned how annoying they could be.

"There you are." Chase hugged me. "I've been looking all over for you. How's the investigation going?"

I sighed and rested my weary head against his shoulder. "It's not going well at all."

"Tell me," he invited.

There were probably some details—like the dirty socks in the sleeping bag—that I should've left out, but I didn't. I told him about the geese and the squishy vegetables. It didn't really make any difference except that I felt better.

"If I can be any help, I managed to get someone to take my joust this afternoon. I'm free for the rest of the day. And I am at your disposal, my lady."

"You're the best." I smiled and kissed him. "No wonder I love you so much."

His dark eyes widened. "Jessie, we haven't been together very long."

My mistake. I kept forgetting our relationship was different here.

"I didn't mean love-love," I qualified. "More like you could love a cinnamon roll or a beautiful gown. Or a sword."

I knew I was babbling, but I didn't want to lose him over a slip of the tongue.

He laughed and took my hand. "Okay. What's your next move?"

"I think I should gather all the castle squires together and see if they know who Jordan worked with last. Doesn't that make sense?"

"Makes sense to me. Let's go."

Because Sir Reginald hadn't suffered a heart attack here, he wasn't in charge of what went on in the castle. He normally would've been the person I'd go to for castle information. Instead when I asked Gus who kept the castle going, he pointed toward the office.

Chase and I went there looking for someone who would know all the squires and could help round them up. We stepped into the office, which in my Village is nothing more than a computer hub.

"Can I help you?" the man behind the desk asked. "I don't see people who wander in off the cobblestones. That's why there are appointments."

I was stunned and thrilled to see my friend, Bart, working through a mountain of paperwork.

"I'm so happy to see you." I started around the desk to hug him.

He held up one massive hand. "I don't know you. Go

back the way you came and find my secretary if you have something to discuss. Good day."

Chase took my arm and whispered, "He's always like this. Everyone hates him. He gets his authority right from Adventure Land and couldn't care less about the Village. Come on."

But I couldn't believe it. Bart and I had been friends almost since we'd met in my Village. His brother had been missing, and he'd come to find him. Chase and I had solved that crime.

Bart made Chase and Canyon look small. He was a giant, the biggest man I'd ever met, and he had the best heart of anyone I knew. This couldn't be all there was to him.

"I'm the Bailiff," I told him. "I need your help solving the two murders that have happened."

His hair was cut very close to his head, unlike the longish style he usually favored. I wondered where he'd found a gray suit big enough to fit him. His clothes were usually tunics and britches—and they had to be specially ordered.

"They've finally lost their minds, haven't they?" He snickered. "A female Bailiff. Crazy."

"Not crazy," I argued. "You think women can do anything. You're in love with Daisy the sword maker. Why not a woman Bailiff?"

"Young woman, you've been out in the sun too long. I don't have a relationship with a sword maker. I think you should leave now."

"You and I have always been friends. It can't be that different here. And you worship Daisy. Think about it. I need your help, Bart."

He rose slowly to his feet, towering over us, making the room feel tight.

"You know there are more security agents in the Village than just the Bailiff, right? Don't make me prove it to you."

Chase kept tugging me toward the door. I finally had to acknowledge defeat.

Out in the corridor, I thought again about these changes. Bart wasn't with Daisy. Roger wasn't with Mary. I'd set both of them up when I knew they really cared about each other. This Village wasn't just influenced by Chase not being the Bailiff. It was also missing my skills as a matchmaker.

But how did that make any difference?

"What were you talking about in there?" Chase asked. "Were you serious about him being with Daisy? Or were you just trying to throw him off?"

"I don't know. I thought maybe I could relate to him in some way. I guess not."

I had to talk with Merlin again. We left the castle but he saw us coming and quickly hid in his apothecary.

"I need you, wizard," I said to him. "You can't hide behind that screen forever. Don't forget that I know who you are."

"Who is he?" Chase wondered. "Someone besides a crazy man in a starred, purple robe?"

"He knows who he is." I'd forgotten that the only reason Chase knew about him being CEO of Adventure Land was because he was Bailiff.

"Go away," Merlin said. "You're ruining everything."

I managed to get across my idea of bringing all the squires together in the castle. Merlin finally looked around the screen he was hiding behind.

"And this is it? You won't keep bothering me?"

"Probably not if you tell Bart to help me."

"All right. But this is it. I won't help again. I don't care who you tell."

Chase shook his head. "What's he talking about?"

"He's the CEO of Adventure Land. He just likes living here." He was going to find out anyway, I reasoned.

"What?" Chase glanced between me and Merlin. "Is that true? How's that possible?"

"That's enough of that," Merlin protested. "You're not supposed to tell anyone if you want my help."

"He won't tell anyone else. Let's go, Chase."

"But he's the head of Adventure Land! There are so many changes we could make—he could help us!"

"Not now!"

We followed the path back up to the castle and waited outside Bart's office as Merlin told him to help us. Chase asked how I'd known about Merlin. What could I say? There was no way to explain.

Bart heaved himself out of the office door. He barely fit through it. He didn't look happy about it either. My Bart would never have looked so angry about such a small request.

"I'm having Marcus gather the squires into the Great Hall," he said. "Please tell me if you need anything else, Lady Bailiff."

"Thank you." I couldn't resist—I was so happy to see him. I ignored that we were strangers and put my arms around him as far as I could reach. "You should talk to Daisy. The two of you will be perfect together. And lose the suit. You aren't office material. I love you, Bart."

To say that he looked shocked was as big an understatement as the man himself. He was so stiff and formal in his suit that I thought he might break in half. I knew I couldn't make all the people here the same as they were where I'd come from. But some things could be made right. This was one of them.

"I don't know what your game is, Bailiff, but I wish you a good day."

Merlin shrugged and went back in the office quickly. Bart squeezed back into the room and slammed the door behind him. I could hear him and Merlin arguing. There was no doubt who the winner would be. Maybe it would be good for the two of them to lock horns. It might make them both better.

Chase went with me to the Great Hall where the King's Feast was held every Sunday night.

"What made you do something like that?" he asked.

"I just couldn't stand to see him that way. He needs

Daisy to help him loosen up."

"Jessie, is there something . . . unusual going on that I should know about?"

"No." I kissed him quickly as a parade of squires began streaming into the Great Hall. "I'm just a little different now. I can't explain it. It's going to be okay. Just trust me."

We took a seat in the area where the king and queen usually sat when they attended the feast. The squires made a line that snaked out the door.

"How many squires are there at the castle?" I asked.

"Dozens. Everyone wants a squire when they stay here. They have to keep extra on staff. It's part of the whole experience."

"Okay. I guess we'll talk to all of them. One of them has to know who sent Jordan to throw away that armor. That's all we have to figure out, right?"

Chapter Eighteen

There were so many squires that they all started to look the same after an hour of interviewing them. It was hard to imagine they could ever need so many, but I knew they didn't have them hanging around for nothing.

The problem was that there was no central clearing house for them—not even a guild like so many of the other groups had. There was a Craft Guild for the craftsmen, an Entertainment Guild—even the pirates had their own guild. Not so the squires. Apparently the Knaves, Varlets, and Madmen's Guild thought the squires felt like they were better than them and had refused them admittance to their guild. At least that's what Chase and I heard from a few squires.

The squires didn't really work together, but they knew each other.

Several of the squires we talked to had spoken with Jordan, but because he was new to the Village, they didn't know much about him. Only a dozen or so were actually full-time squires for specific individuals. The rest worked where they were needed.

Basically, none of them had any idea who Jordan was talking about when he said he'd thrown away someone's armor.

"I feel like a horse ran over me," I said to Chase after we'd spoken to the last squire in line. "How can none of them know anything? That doesn't make any sense."

"I think that's why it's hard for the police to catch the bad guys. Everyone has different ideas and they don't see things the same."

We stood in the Great Hall. It was empty—hard not to appreciate how vast it was with the seating around the arena which hosted jousts, fools, jugglers, camels and horses.

"Let's eat something," Chase said. "I'm starving. I'm sorry this isn't going the way you thought it would. It's exactly my worst nightmare about being Bailiff."

"What?" I asked as we walked out of the hall. "That you couldn't catch the bad guys?"

Chase was very aware of what he was doing and wanted to be good at it. I knew that about him. He didn't like starting anything he wasn't sure he could finish.

"No." He put his arm around me as we walked out of the castle. "That it would take up all my time. I couldn't find someone to take my place at the *Field of Honor* every day, Jessie. Who'd want to do this job 24/7?"

I wasn't expecting that. It was hard to imagine my Chase saying something like that. Maybe this one was too different to ever be Bailiff.

It was cool and dark outside. He didn't like to eat at the castle all the time, so we were headed to the *Lady of the Lake Tavern* a short walk away. The stars were out in dazzling array. The Village was empty except for residents. We heard the sound of laughter and someone practicing their guitar.

The *Lady of the Lake* never sold leftovers from the day like so many of the other restaurants. Most charged half price, some even gave away their leftovers to residents. They knew we didn't make much money, and their hearts were in the Village.

Not so *Lady of the Lake* and a few others like *Polo's Pasta* who either closed when the Main Gate closed or stayed open to charge high prices to the residents.

It was a small crowd at the tavern after hours. People sat in the high-backed, wood booths and talked quietly together. There were no pirate raids as there were during the day for visitors, yet there were several pirates eating, still wearing their costumes.

"Take a seat where you like," Ginny Stewart said without bothering to look up. She owned the tavern. She was a crusty, white-haired, older woman who always wore a slutty green dress which showed her enormous bosom to best effect.

"Thanks, Ginny," Chase said as we walked by her.

That caught her attention.

"Chase! My boy. Where were you at the last joust today? I wasn't the only one disappointed not to find you there."

"I had some things I had to take care of." He hugged her, and she clung to him.

Ginny spared a glance for me. "What's this? Where's Isabelle?"

"We broke up," he briefly explained as we sat in a booth. "This is Lady Jessie. She's the new Bailiff. What's good tonight?"

"A lady Bailiff, eh? If I'd known they were looking for such a thing, I would've put in for it myself. I'd have the steak and kidney pie, if I were you. That's always good."

Her hands were all over Chase as they spoke. That's the way Ginny had always been in my Village too—until she'd died. This was another case, like Wanda and Isabelle, where this woman wasn't alive anymore. It was difficult to look at her, knowing she could be dead soon if this Village followed my own.

I wasn't a fan of steak and kidney pie, so I just had a

salad and some bread. I liked the coarse grain bread Ginny's people made here. It was like a meal in itself.

Two tough-looking pirates got up from their seats and stood beside ours after Ginny had left to get our orders. I didn't recognize them from my time on the *Queen's Revenge*. I thought they might not be in my Village at all.

"So yer the new law in town." The pirate's gold teeth glinted in the lantern light.

"That's right." I wasn't afraid of pirates, not even ones I'd never met. Mostly they were a lot of bluster.

"And who's this?" The second pirate glared at Chase with one eye covered by a black patch with a skull on it. "Is this your pretty lady, Bailiff?"

I got to my feet. "What's your problem? I think you need to go back to your ship before I have to lock you up in the Dungeon."

"We're both so scared we're shaking," the first pirate said.

Chase stood up too, much taller and broader than the pirates. "Maybe you had too much to drink and you didn't understand what the Bailiff said. Go away before you get hurt."

The two pirates glanced at him and slunk away. That made me angry.

"I really need a sword or something. People aren't going to respect me without a weapon."

We sat again in time for Ginny to bring food.

Chase waited until she was gone. "You'll get a reputation after a while. People might not be afraid of you, but they'll respect you."

"Especially when you're with me?"

He covered my hand with his on the table. "It won't be like that—unless you're going to give up being Bailiff when Canyon gets back."

"You mean *if* he gets back. Right now, we don't have anything to prove he didn't kill the fairy or Jordan."

"But he didn't kill the squire," Chase argued. "I think

that's what we should concentrate on. The two were killed in a similar way, right? But we know Canyon was in jail and couldn't kill Jordan."

"But if we can find out who killed Jordan, we might have Apple Blossom's killer too."

"That's right." He put a large spoonful of steak and kidney pie in his mouth and chewed thoughtfully. "What's next? Since we haven't been able to figure out who told Jordan to throw away that armor, where do we go?"

"I don't know." I sighed. Wasn't this enough? Chase and I had a relationship again. We were trying to find the killer together. Why wasn't this over? How much more did it take?

"We'll think of something," he encouraged. "You're going to be the best Bailiff ever."

"Thanks." That wasn't my goal, but I had to settle for it since I couldn't tell him the truth.

We finished eating, almost in peace and quiet, except for Ginny continuing to butt into our conversation. She constantly felt the need to squeeze Chase's arm and put her hand on his back and shoulder.

Dinner was finally over. The tavern was nearly empty. Chase paid for the meal, and we walked out.

"Doesn't that bother you?" I asked him when I was sure Ginny wasn't listening. "She kept touching you. It's as bad as Gus pinching butts."

He smiled as he slipped an arm around me. "Jealous?"

"Annoyed."

"It doesn't bother me. She's a good-hearted woman. She means well."

Yeah. Yeah.

By this time, the guitar player had stopped for the night. I could still hear the elephants bellowing and the camels and horses snorting. The people sounds had mostly vanished as the night had cooled and residents went inside. The wind came from the Atlantic with a strong scent of fish and salt. I could still smell sunblock from visitors who had been there that day.

We didn't talk much as we wandered back to the castle, enjoying each other's company. Most of the castle lights had been turned off for the night leaving pockets of darkness that pooled around us.

The attack came swiftly. Chase groaned and dropped to his knees as someone hit him in the head with something hard. I couldn't tell what it was or who was doing it.

Another person grabbed me and twisted my arms behind me. I struggled, but the person was large and strong—Apple Blossom's killer?

"We don't want no lady Bailiff," a raspy voice said near my ear. "Take care of the camels and the kids who get lost. Let the police take care of the rest."

"Why? Because you killed Apple Blossom and the squire to hide your crime?"

"I'm warning you. Leave it alone."

"No." I knocked my head into his face as I'd frequently had to do to get away from my brother when we were kids. The satisfying *oof* sound came from behind me, and my attacker stepped back.

The two men ran away, vanishing into the darkness. I went to Chase. He was okay, just stunned. My arms felt like they'd nearly been twisted out of their sockets.

"They got away?" Chase asked as I helped him to his feet.

"They did. But one of them is going to have a big bruise on his face tomorrow. I'm pretty sure it was those two pirates from inside."

"They won't be so tough when I see them in the daylight tomorrow."

"Let's get back to the castle. We need to make sure he didn't crack your head open."

"I'm fine. Just feel kind of stupid. I guess I'm good with a pretend sword and lance, but not in a real fight."

"He came up and hit you in the back of the head," I reminded him. "I couldn't believe how loud that thump was. You're lucky you're not unconscious."

He wasn't happy with that assessment and asked Gus if he'd seen anyone unusual hanging around. Gus hadn't seen much of anything since he'd been kissing one of the maids from the castle. We thanked him and went inside to our room.

Another surprise waited for us there. The room had been completely tossed. Someone had gone through what little personal possessions were there, and had stolen Chase's laptop. We called castle security—three men who were more like the Stooges than security guards. They took our statements and left with a promise to return in the morning after they had 'assessed the situation'.

But in the morning, Bart was at our door instead. He was wearing a black suit with a purple tie. It still didn't look right.

"I don't like murder and mayhem in my Village," he said. "What are the two of you doing to cause so much trouble?"

"Looking for the person who killed two people in the Village?" I suggested sarcastically. "Remember when we talked about this yesterday, and you kicked us out of your office?"

He didn't wait to be invited into the room. He came in and leaned against the wall. "I heard you were robbed last night."

"And assaulted." Chase gave him a brief rundown of what had happened between the castle and the tavern.

Bart sighed heavily. "I don't like to get involved in these situations, but you leave me no choice. I'm sure I don't have to tell you how much Adventure Land dislikes this kind of thing."

"We weren't crazy about it either," Chase growled. "What are you going to do to make it different?"

"I have my own way of dealing with unfortunate situations like this. You two go about your normal business, and I'll take care of it."

I felt like we were talking to an oversized Mafia Don. All he was missing was a cigarette and an Italian meal.

"My normal business is finding out who killed these people," I told him. "I'm the Bailiff."

Bart nodded his massive head. "I understand. But I'd like you to simply look after the routine Village events. Am I clear?"

"Sure."

"Don't look at me." Chase picked up his duffel bag. "I'm headed toward the next joust. Let me know if you need anything."

He kissed me and glared at Bart before he left.

"Obviously a disturbed man."

"So what's your plan for finding the killer?" I asked him.

He moved away from the wall. "It doesn't concern you, Bailiff. I'll keep you advised as events unfold."

As he started back out the door, I couldn't resist one more nudge in the right direction. "Have you talked to Daisy?"

"That's another thing that you needn't worry about. I'm perfectly capable of finding this killer and managing my own life. Good day to you, Lady Bailiff."

Chapter Nineteen

When he was gone I sat on the bed and wished really hard that this was over and I was back home. I heard the buzzing of tiny wings before I opened my eyes and saw Starshine next to me.

"I've already told you that I can't change the wish you already wished," she said. "I can grant other wishes if they don't contradict your original wish. I hope that's clear."

"Two people are dead and someone broke into our room last night. That was after they tried to intimidate me and Chase. How much worse does this have to get? Where is the part where you say it's over and it all goes away?"

"I thought I was very specific about what you need to do to go back to your Village."

"Yes. Get Chase to love me, and the two of us solve the murder. But like I said, now there are two murders. How many more do we have to solve?"

"Calm down, Jessie. There is still only one killer. Find him, and you'll go home before you know it."

"You admit there's only one killer?" That was good news. It meant that Canyon had to be innocent. "If you know there's only one killer then you must know who it is. Can't you give me a hint?"

She kicked her feet. "What fun would that be? And what would you have learned from this experience? You know, a fairy godmother's wish is more than just a good time."

"You can say that again."

"I think you know what I mean."

I got up and stalked around the room. It wasn't easy since we were supposed to leave everything a mess until the security people came back. Most of the carpet was full of clutter.

"What's to learn? Chase and I wouldn't be together if he wasn't the Bailiff. I get that. Wanda, Isabelle, and Ginny would still be alive. Roger and Mary wouldn't be together. Neither would Bart and Daisy. And Bart would wear those awful suits and people would hate him."

"Very good." She clapped her hands. "And what conclusion does that bring you to?"

I had to think about it. People were different. My matchmaking skills weren't useful here, or I hadn't used them. What did that have to do with the dead fairy?

"I don't know. The killer is someone different than he is at home?"

"That's true," she agreed.

"And he's looking for a girlfriend? Would I have set him up with someone if Chase had been Bailiff?"

She frowned. "Cold. You've lost the scent."

Our conversation was cut short when the castle security men returned to take samples of everything from toothpaste to carpet. I couldn't figure out what they were doing and was happy when they finally left.

I waited a few minutes for Starshine to return, but she didn't show. Maybe she had other people's lives to mess up.

Eventually I had to hit the cobblestones as my radio began squawking out a dozen problems that needed to be corrected.

This time, I tucked a small dagger into the top of my boot. I didn't want the killer to take me unaware again and someone to end up looking into *my* death. A gun would've been better, but this was Renaissance Faire Village. It would be entirely out of place.

After wrapping the heavy leather belt around my hips, I strode out into the crowded Village, keeping in mind what Chase had said about earning respect. I attacked each situation with renewed vigor and strength. From someone running by and taking King Arthur's sword after he'd pried it from the stone to helping catch Mother Goose's goose, I kept my head high and my confidence higher.

I wasn't sure if the residents of the Village respected me any more by early afternoon, but I was exhausted.

Chase sent a messenger to *Fabulous Funnels* where I was breaking up a fight between two mommies with babies in strollers. They were all dressed as fairies. He had free lunch tickets at the *Pleasant Pheasant*, a restaurant and pub that we liked. I was glad to meet him there.

"Harder than you thought, huh?" he asked as we waited for our late lunch of fish and chips.

I didn't bother lifting my head from the table. "It was much easier when you did it."

"I've never done it."

"Of course you haven't." I rapidly picked my head up and smiled. "I meant it would be easier if you were doing it."

He leaned toward me. "Jessie, you keep saying this weird stuff like you know things the rest of us don't. And you knew things about me that I don't remember ever telling you. What's going on?"

"My fairy godmother brought me to an alternate reality because I wished you weren't the Bailiff anymore so you wouldn't have to find out who killed Apple Blossom. How crazy is that?"

"Pretty crazy," he agreed. "Are you telling me that's

what happened?"

"Of course not. I'm just tired from the new work. I'll get used to it." *Or I'll figure out a way to go home.* "Don't worry about me. How was the joust?"

"It was good. I was surprised to face off against Sir Reginald again. I don't know what he's trying to prove. I don't think he's in bad shape, but he's older. And the *Field of Honor* is rough even when you're not fifty."

"I agree. I'm sure something will happen to make him give it up." *Yeah. Like a heart attack.*

"In the meantime, I can't do my best. I'm afraid of hurting him."

"He's probably going through a midlife thing. Just joust with him like you would anyone else."

Our food arrived, and Chase told me he was going to have to look for yet another squire. The one he'd grabbed when I became Bailiff wasn't working out.

"They have plenty of them at the castle. I'm sure they wouldn't miss one." I told him about the visit from castle security. "They took samples of everything except the leftovers in the fridge."

"There really needs to be a unified security force for the Village and the castle. Probably under the direction of the Bailiff." He smiled at me. "Are you ready for something like that?"

"No. I don't think so. Maybe when Canyon takes the job back again."

"You're giving it up when he gets back?"

Before I could answer, Detective Almond was at our table with Pirate Grigg following him. They both scooted in beside us and ordered lemonade.

"Are you two working the Bailiff job together?" Detective Almond asked. "I hear you got rousted last night and your room was trashed. Anything stolen?"

"Didn't your source tell you that?" I stared at Grigg.

"No. He was out on the lake with the pirates when it happened." Detective Almond frowned. "This wasn't what I had in mind when I said 'undercover'. I was thinking a juggler or a sword swallower."

"All admirable professions," I agreed. "But the pirates get around the Village more than other characters. I was doing my best for him."

"Thank ye."

I almost spewed sweet tea through my nose when I heard the accent Grigg had taken. It seemed some things absolutely remained the same here.

Detective Almond stared at him until Grigg looked away. He was playing with an earring in his newly pierced right ear.

"As I was saying," Detective Almond continued. "You two are highly visible here. The killer seems to know that you're looking for him. It's a good shot that he'll take advantage of it. Fine work."

Chase and I exchanged glances.

"It wasn't what I had in mind," I told him. "I don't think my life is supposed to be threatened as Bailiff."

"It is what it is." Detective Almond shrugged. "What have you got on the squire?"

"Nothing," Chase said. "There are too many of them to figure out what's going on. No one knows who Jordan was working for when he threw away the armor."

"I'm glad you brought that up." Detective Almond took out his notes and perched a pair of reading glasses on the edge of his nose. "The armor Mr. Britt was wearing during your sword fight matches what we're looking for. No blood or semen, but the scratches and kicks from the fairy tell us she fought the man wearing that armor."

"But it wasn't Canyon," I argued. "Surely the dead squire tells us that."

"I tend to agree with you," he said. "The ME says the handprint on the squire's neck was the same size as the one on the fairy's neck. He's hoping to get some fingerprints from their skin, but no luck on that so far."

"So you'll release Canyon?" I asked.

"I think we'll let him go." He put away his notebook. "See what stirs up when he gets back. Maybe nothing, but the killer might want to get rid of him too. If nothing else, he could take his job back as Bailiff again."

I wasn't sure how I felt about that. It was a hard job, but I had the radio. I could spend more time with Chase, but he probably wouldn't feel pushed to become the Bailiff with Canyon in that position.

"We'll see. Thanks for the update," I said. "Has Grigg heard anything about what's going on?"

Grigg heard his name mentioned and suddenly paid attention. "I haven't heard anything, but the pirates are busy right now trying to get the cannon up and running again. It's not as easy as it looks."

He was already going native!

Detective Almond didn't look happy about Grigg's report. "We need to have a talk when we're done here."

"Yes, sir." Grigg's tone lacked its usual snappiness. Instead he sounded more like a whiny teenager.

A call came through on the radio. A woman was riding an elephant and refused to get down. They were calling my name. "I have to go. See you later, Detective."

Chase walked with me. "Good news about them releasing Canyon, huh? He doesn't take the job as seriously as you do."

"And that's a good thing?"

"Good for me." He put his arm around my waist. "Come on, Jessie. You can't really want to be the Bailiff. No one wants that job."

I stopped walking. "Why not? It's an honorable position."

"So is being a knight, and it's a lot more fun."

"Sometimes you have to think about something other than fun." I started walking again.

"I suppose so. But does it have to be you thinking about it? Can't we just let Canyon do what he was doing before?"

"Why can't you see that this is important?"

"Why does it matter to you?"

Oh no. We were having a fight, and we hadn't been together long enough in this place to have a fight. I couldn't risk that part of the equation. Chase and I couldn't break up.

"You're right," I agreed with him. "It would be better for Canyon to take over the job again."

What was I doing? I was always honest with Chase—at least about the important things.

He smiled at me. "That's my girl. We'll be a lot happier without that radio between us."

I gritted my teeth and agreed with him. We had to get the murders resolved before Chase and I had a major meltdown.

Chapter Twenty

I still had to coax the woman off the elephant or at least try to. She'd obviously been out in the sun too long. She wanted to ride the elephant home.

"My house is close by, and I have a two-car garage," she rationalized. "It's mean for you to keep the elephant here. I can take better care of him."

While I was discussing it with her, two of the handlers got up beside her and lifted her off the animal. I'd requested a security guard from the Main Gate, and he escorted her from the Village.

"Thanks, Lady Bailiff." The elephant handler saluted me.

"You're welcome, good sir," I returned.

The line of visitors waiting moved forward slightly as the next children got on the elephant's back.

"Good work," Chase said. "But I like you better as my

squire. Will you come back to the job?"

"Of course," I replied with a quick smile.

It wasn't what I wanted, but all I wanted was to go home. I didn't have time to argue with him. We had to solve the fairy's murder.

We stopped at the blacksmith's shop near the *Field of Honor*. Chase was having new shoes put on his horse. I watched as he and Phil from the *Sword Spotte* talked about swords and knives. Phil was there to oversee the work being done on his new line of swords.

I noticed a large pile of armor in the corner of the area where the forge was. It was almost too hot in there to even pay attention to what they were saying. Still that pile of armor bothered me. Why was it there?

I asked Hans Von Rupp, the blacksmith. He wiped his brow with a blue handkerchief and continued working, banging on metal in the fiery pit.

"The knights bring it in to be repaired. It's not thick metal, so I can take out some dents and patch holes in it. It's cheaper than buying new armor."

"Thanks."

I wondered why the knight who'd had his armor thrown in the trash didn't do this instead. It probably would have taken out the dents that had occurred while he was killing Apple Blossom. Was there something else about the armor that would have given him away?

"Most of the knights at the field use interchangeable armor," Hans said. "Only a few can afford their own armor, like Chase. They usually have something inscribed on it that identifies it as theirs. Chase has his lion on the inside of his chest plate and other pieces. Every well-to-do knight in the Village has their own inscription."

"Really? Like what?"

"Karl has an eagle inscribed in his armor. Milton has a troll in his." Hans took a sword out of the fire. "It has to be on the inside. Everything on the outside has to be plain so they can fight for whoever they serve each day."

"And the squires who serve them would know which inscription belonged to each knight."

"That's right." Hans grinned. "Thinking about getting some armor, Lady Bailiff?"

"She might be if she was going to remain working as the Bailiff." Chase had finished his conversation with Phil. "But Canyon is coming back, and he'll take over those responsibilities."

"Probably for the best." Hans nodded.

The horse was ready to go. We walked him up to the *Field of Honor*. Chase talked about everything except the important things. Those things burned in me. It was all I could do to stop myself from telling him how wrong he was.

Once we reached the stable, he gave his horse to one of the stable boys—or girls. Sometimes it was hard to tell which they were. He slung his arm around my shoulders. That was it.

"I can't believe you told Hans I was giving up being Bailiff," I accused.

"But you are," he insisted. "You said you were going to let Canyon have his job back so we could spend more time together."

I folded my arms across my chest and argued inside about fighting with Chase. It was wrong. If we broke up, I might never go home. I had to smile and take it on the chin.

But I couldn't.

"Don't you get it? Canyon is never going to figure out who killed the squire or the fairy. He doesn't care enough to bother. I'm not giving him the radio or the title until I know what happened."

"I thought you were okay with it," Chase said. "You worry too much. Everything will be fine. If Canyon doesn't figure it out, the police will. I don't know why you're so upset."

I wanted to give him a rational explanation, but the only one I had wouldn't make sense to him. "What about those two men who attacked us last night? Is Canyon going to take care of that too?"

"It was probably just someone fooling around. Come on. Lighten up."

The radio squawked again. Someone had stolen all the chocolate walnut fudge from Frenchy's. How was that even possible?

"They need me. I have to go." I looked into the brown eyes that I loved so much, wishing I could see my Chase in them. But he was a different man. I had to face that.

He nodded and went toward the grandstand as I walked away. I looked back after starting down the hill from the field and saw him talking to Isabelle.

Did I only fall in love with Chase because he was the Bailiff?

"Well of course not." Starshine responded to the question in my heart. "He's a wonderful man—kind, compassionate—you love him for all his traits. Would it have mattered to you if he'd always stayed a knight working at the *Field of Honor*?"

"No. Of course not! But my Chase wouldn't just let this go. He'd want to help, and he wouldn't make stupid remarks about me being Bailiff."

"You're stressed," she said. "You have too much going on in your head. I could send you on a trip to Tahiti for a break."

"No. I'm not going anywhere until I go back to my Village. If you want to help, look for clues or forget I ever wished this stupid wish."

I left her buzzing around outside *Frenchy's Fudge*. I was hoping I could get a good description of the fudge thief, but Frenchy had taken care of it. He'd thrown one of the big, heavy blocks of fudge at the back of the thief's head. It had taken him down. He was still out cold, half in and half out of the shop.

"Good work." I shook his hand. "I'll get him out of the Village."

Frenchy still wasn't happy with that outcome. "I want to

press charges. Two blocks of fudge are ruined. I was up all night making it. I want him to go to prison."

"He won't go to prison for stealing fudge." I tried to reason with him. "What about Vegetable Justice?"

"Vegetable Justice? I want to press real charges against him," he yelled. "He's a thief. In other places, they'd cut off his hands."

I wasn't going through all the trouble to set up Vegetable Justice if Frenchy wasn't happy with it. I called the police department and asked them to have someone meet me at the Main Gate. Stealing fudge would be shoplifting like it was in any department store in the outside world. The kid could get thirty days in the county jail.

"I'm sure the police will let you know when his trial comes up," I said to Frenchy, pulling on the young man's arm as he came around. He wasn't older than his early twenties. "Come on. You're about to be banned from the Village."

The thief came along peacefully. We followed the cobblestones to the Main Gate where visitors were streaming in.

"I just wanted some fudge," he told me. "I didn't know that man would get so upset."

"If you don't want to see it happen again, I suggest you stop stealing."

"Can't you just let this slide? I'll leave. You don't have to turn me over to the police."

He was so young and kind of cute. Like a puppy. I almost did what he asked.

"No, she's not letting you go," a strident voice said from behind me. "You're the same kid who stole that dagger from my place yesterday. I hope the police put you away for a good long while."

It was Daisy Reynolds, the sword maker. She was short and round and always wore a silver breastplate with the image of a phoenix on it. She ignored conventional Renaissance garb for a woman. Her britches were short, and her muscled arms stuck out from her armor.

What would she be like here? She was one of my
favorite people back home. But here she wasn't with Bart.
That probably meant she was different too.

I handed my charge over to the officer who met me at
the side gate. The young man didn't say anything after seeing
Daisy. He went along with the officer, a glum expression on
his poor, cute face.

"Now," Daisy said with a big smile. "We can get some
ale, and you can tell me why you sent Bart looking for me."

I was so happy to see her with her no-nonsense attitude,
Kewpie-doll red lips, and badly dyed blond hair, I even
offered to buy two ales—or at least get them on credit.

We sat in Peter's Pub, out of the hot sun, and sipped our
cool drinks.

"So?" she began. "What's with the matchmaking thing
between me and Bart? And why him of all people? I've never
liked him. Who can like a man who has so much potential
and locks it away in an office every day?"

"I just have a feeling about the two of you. He's
probably not so bad if you get him out of that awful suit."

She giggled, reminding me of a much larger version of
my fairy godmother.

"Jessie, you're a bad girl. No wonder Chase likes you."

I sighed when she said it and took another sip of ale.

"Like that, huh?"

"We had a blow up this morning about me being Bailiff.
He wants me to give the job back to Canyon. I'm not ready to
do that."

"Just stand your ground," she advised. "And don't let it
bother you. He'll come around. Or he won't. If not, he's not
the man I think he is."

I told Daisy about the murder investigation. "I just found
out that every piece of armor that belongs to a knight in the
Village is marked with their particular sigil."

She nodded. "That's right. When I make armor, I have to
consult the Big Book of Knights if they forget to tell me what

their sigil is. It's a big deal around here."

"The Big Book of Knights?"

"Yes. They keep it up at the castle. No two knights can have the same sigil. Of course that's the upper crust. The knights who are only visiting or rent their armor are different."

"That could be my answer. I couldn't find out whose armor the police had confiscated from Canyon. I knew it wasn't his—it's the good stuff. The squires didn't know who Jordan was working for when he threw it away. But if we take a look at the sigil inside, we could compare it to the Big Book of Knights, and we'd know who it belonged to."

Daisy ordered another round of ale. "I don't know. What you just said started to give me a headache right away."

I laughed and hugged her, even though I knew she hated it. "I'm going to the police station to take a look, and I'll compare it to the Big Book of Knights. Maybe then this will be over."

"Sounds good. I'd go with you, but uniforms and I don't get along. Let me know when you get back. I think Bart is in charge of the Big Book of Knights. Maybe I could help persuade him to let us take a peek."

I debated about changing clothes before I went to the station. They tended to act different with Rennies. I needed information, not harassment. I'd given my street suit to the laundry at the castle. I didn't know if it was ready.

But I had not considered the efficiency of the castle staff.

By the time I got back, my suit was hanging in Chase's closet, clean and pressed, and the rooms were clean again. I changed quickly and did what I could with my hair before looking under every piece of furniture for shoes. I finally found them in the bathroom of all places. I was as ready as I could be to go into the real world.

Someone came into the rooms without knocking. Thinking it could be whoever had broken in earlier—I hid in the alcove behind the bathroom door and waited. It only took a minute for me to figure out that it was Chase and not an intruder. He'd probably come back to change clothes before lunch. Sometimes the heat and dust got the better of all the knights.

I was about to let him know that I was there when the door to the suite opened again. This time it was Isabelle.

"I'm so glad I found you," she said in a tearful voice. "I just hate that we've broken up, don't you? It can't be over between us, Chase. Not yet."

"Isabelle. You know I care about you. I always will. But there's something really special about me and Jessie together. Maybe it doesn't make sense—I don't always understand it."

"What do you see in her? She's tall and gawky. She dresses like a man. And what in the world makes her hair look that way? Why would you rather be with her when you could be with me?"

There were some not-so-subtle smooching sounds. I could imagine Isabelle winding her arms around Chase. I was glad I couldn't see it.

"I'm sorry," he finally said. "I'm with her now. I don't want to hurt you. Try to understand."

"I understand," she raged, knocking over something that shattered on the floor.

Like we didn't have enough of that already.

"You won't be happy with her," she said. "And I won't be waiting for you to crawl back to me. I hope you understand that, Chase Manhattan. You are officially out of my life."

He didn't say anything. The door closed. I wasn't sure if I should admit that I'd heard what they'd said. I waited, feeling time ticking away for me to go to the police station and get back.

"You may as well come out now," he said. "I guess Isabelle didn't notice, but I see your Bailiff's belt on the bed, Jessie."

I came around the bathroom door. "Sorry. I didn't know that would happen. I thought you might be the person who broke into our room."

Chase wrapped his arms around me and kissed me for several moments.

"What was that for?" I asked breathlessly when I could.

"That was to say I'm sorry for being a jerk this morning. I let other things cloud my judgement."

"Okay. You're forgiven."

"Where are you off to?"

I told him about looking up the individual sigils to be found on armor from knights in the Village. "Want to come?"

"I thought you'd never ask."

Chapter Twenty-one

It took much longer than I'd planned.

I was dressed, and then I wasn't. Chase had to change clothes. The whole thing was much more complicated—and enjoyable—than I'd thought it would be.

Grabbing my cell phone, we were finally on our way out of the castle when we ran into Canyon on his way back into the Village.

"Jessie!" He greeted me, wiping tears from his eyes. "I've been looking for you everywhere."

He came toward me with his arms open, and I sidestepped, grabbing Chase's arm instead. He had to know how I felt and acknowledge it like Isabelle had.

"So that's how it is." His big blue eyes were pitiful. "Fine. I'm out of jail now. Somebody said you've been Bailiff while I was gone." He glared at Chase.

"Not me." Chase shrugged. "She's your local law

enforcement."

"What? A girl can't be the Bailiff." Canyon snorted as he laughed. "That's just weird."

"Weird or not." I bristled. "I have the radio and the belt. I'm the new Bailiff."

Canyon was nearly lost for words. "Well I still have the Dungeon. I'm not moving out. I'm going to talk to the king, if I have to. I want my job back."

"I guess we'll see." I walked by him, tugging Chase to walk with me.

I could feel Canyon watching us as we left. I had no doubt he would make good on his threats to get his job back. I had to make this work.

Chase and I stopped for lunch before we went to the police station. He was always hungry. The cheeseburgers, something we couldn't get at the Village, were delicious. We'd sneak out regularly to stop at this one restaurant. It was our place.

After that, we went to talk to Detective Almond. He showed us the evidence room where the red and black armor had been stashed. Chase took it apart carefully as we searched for a sigil. I was worried that it might turn out to be another dead end, belonging to no one in particular.

But there it was, finally, inside the helm.

"A flower?" Detective Almond asked. "What's the significance of that?"

"It's a Scottish thistle." I snapped a picture of it. "It's been used by royalty forever. The thistle has been the national emblem of Scotland since a barefoot Viking stepped on one as he was sneaking up on the Scots army. He yelled so loud that the army woke up and defended themselves. Now it's considered good luck."

Detective Almond stared at me. "Did you just make that up, or is it a real thing?"

"I was a history professor. It's a real thing. And it might help us catch the killer."

"I'll hang on to the armor just in case," he said. "Let me

know what you find out."

We got back in the car, and Chase pulled out into traffic.

"I can't imagine whose armor that could be. Everyone I know with personal armor has some kind of animal like a wolf or a bear. Who'd want a thistle?"

"Someone who knew what it meant, obviously." I studied the picture of the engraving on my cell phone. "We'll see if Daisy knows the answer. If not, we'll go for the Big Book of Knights."

"The Big Book of Knights." He nodded. "You have to get special permission for that."

"I think I can manage it." I thought about Daisy and Bart. That would be one good thing I could leave behind in this place.

Would this Village still be here when I was gone? That was a question that made me feel crazy. Would there be another Jessie, or would Chase be alone, wondering what had happened to me? I would have to ask my fairy godmother when I saw her again.

The Village was crowded when we got back. The line for the hatchet throw snaked down a few blocks away from the game. Women were cooling themselves with pretty painted fans as they waited in line for their turn. Even though the afternoons were hot, many visitors came after spending the morning at the beach. It was our best time of day.

"I have to get changed and get up to the field for the joust," Chase said as we reached the castle. "You could wait to look at this until I get back."

"Or maybe I can find the killer, and we'll celebrate tonight."

"That sounds promising too. Just watch your back. Both of these murders have taken place during the day with hundreds of people around. Stay safe."

"You too." I kissed him. "Watch your front too."

We went our separate ways. I found Daisy at her sword shop, working on a complex design for an expensive sword hilt. I told her about the thistle and she looked at her records.

"I've never encountered that one before." She shook her head. "Looks like we'll have to see Bart."

"You sound happy about it."

"He's a big fella." She grinned. "I like 'em big."

We laughed as we started back along the cobblestones. Her shop, *Swords and Such*, was part of *Armorer's Alley*, a group of shops that specialized in armor and weaponry. It was close to the *Field of Honor*. I could hear the loud *Huzzahs!* from there.

But then people started screaming. I took a quick look at Daisy and turned back to cut through the alley to reach the *Field of Honor* faster. She followed behind me at a slower speed, huffing anyway. Daisy had strong arms but wasn't much of a sprinter.

Something was wrong. My sense of alarm was born out when hundreds of people came running from the field. A few of them were nearly trampled beneath the feet of those trying to get away. I helped as many as I could and then left the rest to Daisy. I was concerned about Chase.

I saw at once what the problem was. One of the knights—possibly the one facing Chase in the joust—had lost control of his horse and had plunged into the spectators. The sheer weight and force of the galloping animal had snapped the fence and destroyed the first few rows of bleachers. It looked as though visitors were trapped in what was left.

My radio squawked out a warning. Better late than never, I supposed. I scanned the field, searching for Chase. I saw his horse, and the squire leading it away, but there was no sign of him.

I headed toward the spectators. A few had cuts and scrapes. There was some blood on the ground. The horse might have been the one with the worst injuries. The large gray mare was on her side, possibly with broken forelegs. I wasn't a vet, but I immediately called for the vet on duty who worked at the field.

That was when I saw Chase. He was under the bleachers handing injured people out to others who could get them away from the scene. He had two chubby, blond toddlers in his big arms. They were crying, but he was intent on trying to get their minds off what had happened by joking with them and making funny faces.

I smiled. This was my Chase. I knew he was in there somewhere.

Everyone who worked for the Village was trying to help out. Jugglers, knaves, and squires were all pitching in. It was wonderful to see everyone together, trying to make a difference.

Canyon showed up as he walked alongside the ambulance making sure everyone stayed out of the way. The Bailiff's job, to be sure, but I didn't feel like arguing the point.

Daisy and I were with four frightened children who'd lost their parents in the mad flight to get away from the horse.

"Should we take them to the police?" She was holding a crying two-year-old in her arms.

"I'm sure they'll come to us. The parents are bound to notice they're missing soon. I think we should stay where we are."

She swiveled her head, searching the crowd that was building instead of getting smaller. "How do you run away and not take your kid?"

I saw one parent running toward us with tears streaming down her face. She was holding one young boy's hand and had a baby in a pack on her chest.

"I guess that's how." I nodded toward her.

The mother was so relieved to find her young daughter. "Thank you so much. I thought she was with me. She's not hurt, is she?"

"No. She seems fine. Paramedics will be here in a moment if you'd like to have them take a look at her." I pointed to the ambulance that was slowly making its way toward us.

All the missing parents showed up, the other three sets

with less reason to have lost their children, but I tried not to judge. It had to be a terrifying moment when the horse jumped into the bleachers. Panic made people do strange things.

A few of the visitors were swearing they would sue the Village. That was nothing new. If a person broke a fingernail while they were here, they were likely to get a lawyer and file a lawsuit. That was modern America encroaching into our Renaissance world.

After I was relieved of my childcare responsibilities, I went to find Chase. He was with his young opponent, the Village vet, and the injured horse. The would-be knight was crying more than any of the parents who'd misplaced their children.

"Is she going to be okay?" I asked Chase.

The horse was still down while the vet carefully examined her.

"We think so. It doesn't look like she broke anything—except the bleachers." Chase put his arm around me. "Everything else okay?"

"Yes. People came back for their children. I didn't see more than some cuts and bruises, but you never know. I'm glad that's not part of my job to decide who's really hurt and who's faking it."

"She's a little bruised, but she's going to be fine," the vet told the young man who'd been riding the mare.

"I shouldn't have brought her here. I don't know what I was thinking." He wiped tears from his face.

"Excuse me." Chase kissed the side of my head and went to speak with the young man.

The problem seemed to be that the horse hadn't come from our stable. The rider had brought her with him. This kind of thing happened sometimes when the rider and horse weren't approved before going on the field. Only an experienced rider and a well-trained horse should have been out there jousting, but it happened sometimes in my Village too.

And maybe the mare and her rider were both well-trained, but strange things occurred that couldn't be planned for. I'd seen it plenty of times.

Chase wanted to stay and help with cleanup. The field was shut down. No more jousts that day. I was eager to see the Big Book of Knights and find out who the killer was. Daisy offered to come with me. Even though I knew she and Bart were bound to end up together, I was still surprised by her eagerness to flirt with him.

"What? You don't think an older broad like me can get some kicks out of finding a new lover?" She winked and grinned. "Better think again."

"Do I hear wedding bells in the future? I love big Renaissance weddings."

"Save it for yourself, Jessie. I was married once. I'm not doing it again. Not the marrying kind, I guess. Did I ever tell you I have a kid? He didn't grow up with me. What do I know about raising a child? But I've always kept my eye on him. I knew about him even if he didn't know about me."

I pretended to be surprised, but in my Village, Daisy's son worked with her at *Swords and Such*. So did Bart. And he never wore a suit and tie.

But I wasn't here to correct that problem. Chase was in love with me and well on his way to becoming the next Bailiff. All we needed now was the killer in jail. That should be enough to send me home.

Thousands of people were streaming out of the Village after the incident at the *Field of Honor*. No doubt most of them didn't even know what had happened. They were just reacting to seeing the police cars and the ambulance rolling down the cobblestones. Nothing like that kind of reality to ruin a day in the Renaissance.

"Probably just as well they're getting out of here." Daisy looked up at the sky. "I think a storm is brewing."

I agreed with her, seeing the flashes of lightning in the clouds coming toward us.

"We better move if we want to get to the castle before

we get soaked."

"This is the only speed I have," she told me.

"You were running back there at the field," I teased her.

"And that was my exercise for the day. Maybe for the week. These little legs weren't meant for running. But you run on if you want. I'll see you when I get there. Just don't talk to Bart. You've already got your man."

I didn't leave her. Daisy and I were good friends in either Village. I enjoyed talking to her about her work. We discussed whether or not I should let Canyon go back to being Bailiff again.

"He does a good job," she said. "As long as he doesn't have to think too much."

I couldn't help wondering if Canyon was the same in my Village. Had I missed that when I'd hired him, or was it just that he was different here?

Gus was at the castle door like always. He was on his best behavior as a group of school kids were touring the castle. I was surprised to see Isabelle leading that tour. I'd never known her to do anything that useful.

She stared at me in a cold, calculated kind of way. I didn't blame her—I had stolen Chase from her. I'd probably feel the same way if our positions were reversed.

"You're lucky she doesn't have laser vision," Daisy remarked after we passed the tour group. "You'd be burned up by now."

"I know. But she'll get over it. There's always another prince or lord who wants her."

"People could've said that about you a few years back too."

"Yeah. But not since I fell in love with Chase. He's it now."

We'd reached Bart's office. Daisy fussed with her hair and asked me how she looked. She looked as she always did—like a pretty, chubby doll. I knocked on the door when she was ready, and we confronted Bart's secretary in the tiny outer office.

"Do you have an appointment?" she asked.

"Yes," I lied. "I'm the Bailiff. He's expecting me."

The secretary buzzed us through the door. Bart was behind his desk, but he wasn't wearing a suit. Instead he'd found a forest green doublet and brown britches that barely reached his knees. He had a leather jerkin and belt over the doublet. He didn't look like the same person.

"Come in. Come in." He heaved himself up from the chair and came to greet us—Daisy in particular. "I'm so glad to see you."

When had all this happened? I was happy for them but amazed that he'd changed so completely since yesterday.

Daisy smiled up at him. "You look so much better in those clothes. I can't tell you."

"You like them?" He peered down at himself. "It was Jessie. She suggested it. I never thought about dressing this way. I thought I should wear a suit even though this is Renaissance Village."

"You look great," I said. But he only had eyes for Daisy.

The couple stared at one another as they held hands. I didn't want to be the one to disturb them, but I really wanted to take a look at the Big Book of Knights.

Daisy finally snapped out of it. "Oh. That's right. We're here to see the Big Book of Knights. Jessie found a Scottish thistle sigil in the armor the police confiscated. You know anyone who uses that?"

"Not me. I glanced through the book, but I wasn't really paying attention. I'd rather read an electronic copy than one made of paper."

"Does this go all the way back to the start of the Village?" I asked.

"Yes. I'll get it for you." He sighed when he looked back at Daisy. "You look beautiful today. I wonder if I could take you out for dinner."

"Sure thing." She grinned. "I love free meals."

"Me too."

I had to pull them apart as they continued to gaze into

each other's eyes, but it was nice to see them together at last.

The Big Book of Knights was really big. It was aptly named for a weighty tome. I wasn't sure who had started recording all the knights from the Village, their sigils, weapons, and who they fought for. It had to be a huge undertaking.

"There you are." Bart opened the black, leather-bound book on a podium. "It has to stay here for security reasons, and I'm afraid the spine would break if you tried to move it."

"That's fine. I don't mind looking through it here."

Bart and Daisy adjourned to his office. I stayed in the library/computer room with the Big Book of Knights.

In the beginning, someone had large, round handwriting and wrote dozens of pages about each knight. It not only included who they were and their sigil, but also their favorite foods and what they wore. There was enough information to use as a dissertation all by itself.

After the first dozen or so knights, someone else took over the responsibility for the book. This person carefully printed the information and limited it to what really mattered for the knight's history.

Even so, it was difficult to follow. The information skipped around from knight to knight. Sometimes I wasn't sure which knight it was talking about.

The next historian was even briefer. They listed the knight's name, sigil, and who they fought for in a clear concise style. There were no dates. I couldn't tell which knights were still there at the Village, if any.

I was surprised to see Roger's name in the list. He'd jousted for a summer after becoming a police officer. It was probably a hobby for him. I knew he liked horses. Most of the knights did. His sigil was a gryphon. No wonder he'd named his shop the *Glass Gryphon*.

Most of the sigils were strong animals such as large birds, lions, tigers and even an elephant. Some were magical creatures such as dragons and wizards. There was one knight, Sir Francis, whose sigil was a unicorn. I'd never met him, but

I felt sure he was an interesting person.

. The knights that had been at the Village when I'd first started coming were mostly gone. I recognized a few names, though many of them had opened shops in the Village and stopped jousting.

My brother, Tony, was listed there too. His sigil was a hawk. I knew he'd jousted for a while. I'd never even known he had a sigil—or his own armor. How had he afforded it?

Sir Dwayne, who had been one of Isabelle's many lovers, had a jackal as a sigil. Sir Marcus Bishop, who had fought for the queen in many jousts, used the wolf sigil.

I finally had my 'AH-HA!' moment when I found a knight who used the Scottish thistle as his sigil. And then, just as quickly, I was deflated.

Daisy and Bart were kissing in his office. I ignored them.

"I thought there was only one knight per sigil. There are two knights with the Scottish thistle. What's up with that?"

Chapter Twenty-two

Daisy sat up and blinked at me. Bart completely ignored me.

"That's not possible. It was never supposed to be that way."

"Take a look in the Big Book of Knights," I invited. "Two men share the Scottish thistle."

Bart grudgingly got up and followed us into the library/computer room. All three of us studied the book.

"She's right," he said. "Sir Reginald uses the thistle, and so did Lord Dunstable."

"But Dunstable hasn't jousted in years," Daisy argued.

"That doesn't mean he didn't kill the fairy and the squire wearing his old armor," I said. "Sir Reginald shouldn't be jousting anymore either. He's getting kind of old for it."

"There isn't an age restriction on participating in Village events," Bart said. "A lord or lady could joust until they were ninety, if they so desired."

"Which doesn't really solve my problem," I reminded the two love birds. "Which man is responsible for the murders?"

Sir Reginald and Lord Dunstable had already been at the Village for years when I'd first visited. Both men were large and probably strong enough to strangle Apple Blossom and the young squire. They both lived in the castle. It was difficult to say which man could also be a killer.

"Neither of them," Bart said. "I've worked with both of them in my daily routines. While they might both be arrogant, and sometimes set in their ways, neither man is a killer."

"But the thistle was engraved in the armor, sweetie," Daisy reminded him. "It has to be one of them. I think either one would consider himself above the fray enough to get rid of someone if they wanted to."

"It's just an engraving," he said. "Any sigil could be engraved in a suit of armor. I know these men. They aren't killers."

"I guess I have to side with Daisy. Whoever killed these people knew the Village very well. Lord Dunstable and Sir Reginald are brazen enough to consider doing it during the day around thousands of people. That takes a special kind of person."

"How are you going to know which man it was?" Daisy asked.

"We should ask them," Bart concluded. "Give them a chance to answer the question as you would any man. Honesty should always be trusted."

Daisy pinched his cheek. "You're from another world, aren't you? We obviously need to lay a trap for them."

"I can't be part of that kind of deceit," he added.

"That's fine. I'll come get you for dinner. Me and Jessie will figure this out. But keep your mouth closed. We don't need anyone finding out what we're doing before we spring our trap."

We left Bart still protesting about human rights.

"What do you have in mind?" I asked her.

She shrugged. "I don't know. You're the Bailiff."

"I can't think of anything to trap either one of those men."

"We have to figure out why the fairy was killed since she was the first victim," Daisy said. "Any idea what caused that?"

"Absolutely none." I couldn't tell her that I'd been spending most of my time trying to get Chase to fall in love with me. "We've been too busy trying to get Canyon out of jail."

"I might know someone who can help with that," Daisy said. "She's new to the Village, but I like her. Come with me."

It had already occurred to me that not having a heart attack could have caused Sir Reginald's personality to change. On the other hand, Lord Dunstable was still overseeing the jousts at the *Field of Honor*. That meant he was different too. Both men had similar personalities, as far as I was concerned. Straight-laced. Arrogant. Pompous. A little too sure of their importance in the Village.

But could that lead to murder?

I followed Daisy back down into the Village. It was barely six p.m., but all the visitors were gone. There weren't even any stragglers that had to be asked to leave for the night, a rare occurrence. All that remained were residents and maintenance people getting an early jump on their work. No doubt the story of the horse crashing through the fence had made the news. Attendance might be down for a day or two.

Funny how that worked. Murder drew crowds. Accidents made people stay home. I never pretended to understand.

"Where are we going?" I finally asked as we walked by Mirror Lake on the way to the other side of the Village near the Main Gate.

"I told you—she's an old friend of mine who's in line to get a shop. They didn't have anything available but offered her a tent until something comes up. You'll like her. We've known each other for years. She has a good understanding of people and how they work. She's got a PhD in psychology or some such."

"So she's going to open a shop as a psychologist in the Village?" I was trying to imagine how that would fit in. How would she make money talking to people about their problems?

"Nah. That wouldn't work. She's gonna deck herself out as a fortune teller," she said as we approached the elegant purple and gold Renaissance-style tent that hadn't been there the last time I'd walked by this spot. "She's gonna call herself Madame Lucinda. What do you think?"

I wasn't sure if I was happy to see her here or not. She was far more than a psychologist masquerading as a fortune teller in my Village.

Daisy pushed aside one of the tent flaps. "Lucy? Are you here?"

We walked into the main area of the thick tent. The same tables held crystal scrying balls, and otherworldly paraphernalia. The small green dragon with yellow eyes was perched on a shelf where she could view the room.

But the dragon didn't move. I walked over and touched it. The eyes stayed fixed.

"Hello. I'm not quite open for business." Madame Lucinda walked through the tent flap that I knew led to a smaller room. She was dressed in her usual purple robe but with one significant difference—she was completely human.

Madame Lucinda at my Village was part dragon.

She's never confirmed it, but I've seen her heavily-scaled, squat, dragon leg. The rest of her looked normal. This fortune teller wasn't anything but a woman with a degree in psychology who wanted to work in the Village and had come up with a routine like everyone else.

I was relieved. Not that I don't like Madame Lucinda—the one who's part dragon. She's a wise woman. I'm a little nervous with her dragon, Buttercup, but otherwise, she's okay.

"Hi Lucy." Daisy smiled when she saw her. "We have a little problem I thought you might be able to help with."

We sat at the round table and explained the situation to her. I couldn't stop myself from glancing at the small dragon every few seconds. I was so used to it looking back and moving around. It didn't do anything this time. I was just being paranoid.

"It sounds to me like you have a frustrated killer on your hands," she said. "I'm assuming it's a man from your description of the crime. Sometimes men feel that they've lost part of their lives as they age. Women do too, but not in the same way men do. Men feel the urge to prove their virility. That may have been the case with the young fairy. When your victim refused to help your killer prove his masculinity, he turned on her with no thought of the consequences."

"Wow." Daisy laughed. "I knew we should come to you."

"How do we catch this person?" Lord Dunstable and Sir Reginald could both fit the bill the way she was describing the killer.

"You should appeal to his vanity," she advised. "Offer him something that will prove he's still a young and virile man."

Daisy glanced at me. "All we need is another fairy to use as bait."

"Bait?" I asked. "You mean stake her out with a sign that says come get me? Because otherwise he has his pick of pretty young fairies every day."

"If I may suggest something more overt," Madame Lucinda said. "Send someone to him and then have her reject him. Since it probably appears to him that he's gotten away with the first two crimes, another death won't be as difficult for him."

I really wanted something easier and safer. Maybe something I could spray on each of them and the real killer would show himself. But that really was fantasy.

"Apple Blossom had a friend, Stacie—I mean Blueberry." You gotta love those fairy names. "I think she might be willing to help."

"Sounds good to me. But which one do we start with?" Daisy asked.

To me there was no question, but then I knew Sir Reginald had been spared a heart attack in this Village. He was still jousting instead of minding the castle. No doubt in my mind that he needed to prove himself.

"We'll start with Sir Reginald. I'll call Detective Almond and get the blueberry fairy's phone number." I smiled at Madame Lucinda. "Thanks for your help."

"It was a pleasure." She smiled and shook my hand. Her hands were normal too, warm, and smooth.

"Let's get on with it." Daisy got up from her chair. "I'd like to get this off Bart's table so he and I can talk about the important stuff." She winked at me.

I glanced up for the last time at the small dragon before I followed her.

"Jessie?" Madame Lucinda called before I could escape the tent. "I notice you've taken quite a shine to my baby dragon."

"Let's just say, this is Renaissance Village. Anything is possible."

"But not the Village you come from, is it?"

Oh no. "I don't know what you mean." And I didn't plan to admit anything.

"That's fine." She smiled. "I understand. Good luck with your plan."

"Thanks." I peeked at the baby dragon once more. Were his golden eyes glowing? And hadn't his tail been on the other side?

I hurried out of the tent and caught up with Daisy.

"I'm going to check on where Sir Reginald is supposed to be this evening," she said. "Bart keeps up with all that. Have you called Detective Almond yet?"

"No. I haven't had a chance."

"What were you doing back there?" she demanded. "Do you want to catch the killer or not?"

I took out the radio, but before I could use it, Chase found us.

"Ladies." He put his arm around our shoulders and kissed the side of my face. "What brings you out on such a nice evening?"

"We were talking to the new fortune teller," Daisy said. "We've got a plan to catch the killer."

"Count me in," he said. "What do we have to do?"

Chapter Twenty-three

When Chase heard the plan, he was completely against it. "You can't control the variables in the situation. We don't have a microphone the blueberry fairy can wear so we know when she's in trouble. We could wait too long, and she could be dead."

Daisy contemplated his words. "I guess we would've caught him in the act then, right?"

He stared at her in disbelief.

I didn't think the plan sounded that bad. If Stacie/Blueberry was willing to give it a try, who were we to keep her from finding her friend's killer?

"That's the best we could come up with," I told him. "Do you have something better?"

"No, but that doesn't make it a good plan."

"Come on," Daisy urged. "Let's see what Bart has to say. Jessie, call Detective Almond and get that phone number."

Unfortunately, Bart agreed with Chase. "That could be really dangerous. I can't be part of a plan that could end up with someone dead in the castle. I could lose my job."

"Dead in the water then, I guess." Daisy slumped in a chair. "I don't suppose you have a better plan?"

"Who could have a plan for something like this?" Bart asked. "I shouldn't have taken off my suit. Things have been falling apart since then."

"I'm not disagreeing that we need a plan to figure out if Dunstable or Sir Reginald are guilty of murder," Chase conceded. "I'm only saying that we need a better plan so no one gets hurt."

"How about if we start with where both men are tonight?" Daisy suggested.

We all looked at Bart.

"Okay. I can do that—as long as we're not dangling a fairy as bait." He consulted an appointment book almost the size of the Big Book of Knights. "Lord Dunstable is at the castle this evening having dinner with the king and queen."

"And Sir Reginald?" I asked.

"He's here having dinner alone." Bart grinned. "So neither one of them are going to kill any fairies, saying your theory is correct. We have time to plan something else."

We sat around in Bart's office trying to come up with something. Since I was convinced that the killer was Sir Reginald, my ideas came firmly down to trapping him. I couldn't explain my reasoning to them without giving away why I was here.

For whatever reason, Daisy seemed to feel the same way about Dunstable. Our ideas clashed because of it.

"Why not find a young castle wench to take Lord Dunstable to her room for an after dinner treat?" she suggested. "We could doll her up some and see what happens."

"That's the same as the fairy," Chase said. "Unless you want to tell her that we're using her to catch a killer."

"The only one likely to sign on for that is a police woman," she told him. "And I don't think we have any of those here."

Detective Almond returned my call after I'd left him voicemail. He gave me Stacie/ Blueberry's real name, her address, and phone number. I thanked him and evaded his questions as to why I wanted that information.

"Have you got something going on out there I should know about?"

"No," I answered honestly since our plan had been scrapped. "I just thought I might ask her if she had other details."

He mulled that over. "All right. Just don't do anything stupid without me."

I had to put my hand to my lips to keep from laughing. Enough of a sound must have escaped to make him realize that I was having fun with his answer.

"You know what I mean. What's with you anyway, Jessie? Canyon never laughed when I said things he didn't understand."

"I'm sorry. I'll talk to you later, unless we decide to do something stupid. Then you're at the top of my call list."

"You shouldn't tease him that way," Bart said after I'd put my phone back in my pocket.

"She might as well," Daisy said. "He can take it. I remember when he was Bailiff and he made us call him 'The Constable'. He didn't have a sense of humor back then either."

"I'm getting hungry." Chase glanced at his watch. "Why don't we talk about this while we eat? Double date?"

Bart nodded eagerly. "That sounds good. I heard Baron's has people from the Merry Mynstrels playing tonight—and two for one brats."

"That's my fella." Daisy grinned. "A romantic evening of beer and brats."

I wasn't comfortable leaving the castle with no plan in the works. I reminded Chase and my friends that Sir

Reginald could strike again if he was rebuffed. "Just like Madame Lucinda said."

"Who?" Chase asked.

"She's new," Bart replied. "But Sir Reginald has managed to go more than one night without killing anyone. I think we're probably safe having dinner."

"Why are you so dead set on it being Reggie?" Daisy wondered. "I've always found Dunstable to be a lot more repugnant."

"I don't know. Just something about him." I hesitated. "I guess you're right. Going out to dinner will probably be fine. It would take Sir Reginald or Lord Dunstable a while to build up to getting rejected again, right? Let's go for the brats."

We walked down the hill together from the castle. Because the night was fair, there were dozens of residents out perfecting their performances. The green man was on his stilts, careening across the cobblestones. A few mad men were still out asking for pennies in their pots as they banged them around. A sword swallower was working on his act. I couldn't look. It always made me cringe.

The warm evening was filled with music and laughter. A crowd had gathered outside Daron's. The eating establishment was too small to seat so many people. Dozens of residents sat on the grass with their food.

We waited in line for thirty minutes before we got inside and were handed a wood platter with two brats and a tankard of beer. The musical trio featured a guitar, a mandolin, and a banjo—the banjo not being part of Renaissance history but acceptable after the Village had closed.

Chase found us a soft patch of grass near the swan swing, one of our favorite places in my old Village. We sat under the stars and ate like kings and queens. It was wonderful.

It made me wish this was the real thing, and wonder what Chase was doing in the other Village without me. Did he even realize that I was gone? My mood deteriorated rapidly after that until I was as melancholy as the dark romantic music being played by the trio inside.

I got a call on the radio about a disturbance at *Stage Caravan*. Of course it was all the way across the Village from where we were. I was tempted to ignore it.

Chase and Bart were in line again waiting for more beer and brats. Daisy was talking to a knight about buying a new sword from her. I finally convinced myself to go after the second alert. I was only sitting here feeling sorry for myself anyway. I might as well see what the problem was.

Since Daisy was the closest, I told her I was going and would be back soon. She nodded but kept haggling with the knight over the price of the sword.

I crossed the cobblestones and headed for *Stage Caravan*. But the sprinklers were already on for the night, so I had to zigzag around the Village Green on the King's Highway, past the *Mother Goose Pavilion* and the *Pleasant Pheasant*, which was surprisingly closed for the night.

Stage Caravan was primarily dancing girls in skimpy costumes and rhythmic music. Things could get a little crazy there sometimes, particularly after hours when the dancing continued and a few residents got drunk and out of hand.

It wasn't a big deal usually. I couldn't ever remember Chase being gone long when he was called to stop a problem there. I could see the colored lanterns swaying in the light breezes by the time I'd passed the blacksmith's shop. I heard the loud music and laughter—definitely a party. If they'd brought it over to Baron's, no one would've noticed. But there were several large housing units for residents on this side of the Village. No doubt one of them had called it in.

I watched the dancers on stage, thinking about the time my brother, Tony, had become infamous here as a sexy dancer. I hoped that wasn't this time. The things that happened in this Village were slightly different than the things that had happened in my Village. It could be confusing.

But I couldn't really understand why anyone had reported the dancers and musicians on stage. They weren't rowdy or all that noisy. Sure, they were having a birthday party for one of the dancers, but I didn't think it was that bad.

How did Chase make those decisions? A complaint was still a complaint. Could I just ignore it?

"Thank goodness you're finally here, Bailiff." Sam Da Vinci approached. "What took you so long?"

I seemed to remember that Sam lived over this way. He had his own place—a small, thatched roof cottage. He was usually easy to get along with. Maybe he had company, and the sound from the stage was bothering him.

"I came as soon as I could, but the stage noise isn't really that bad. I don't think it was worth a complaint."

"I'm not talking about the music from the stage," he said. "Something is wrong with the Dungeon. I can hear those stupid fake prisoners moaning and crying. That's supposed to stop when the Village closes. How am I supposed to sleep with that racket?"

I hadn't even noticed the sounds coming from the Dungeon until he'd pointed it out. I was listening to the music and trying to decide if it was too much. Once he'd mentioned it, I could hear the prisoners screaming and calling for help. I knew what he meant—sometimes the Dungeon soundtrack got left on after Chase and I were in bed for the night. It wasn't something I wanted to listen to while I was going to sleep either.

"Sorry. I'll take care of it."

"If you're the Bailiff, why is Canyon still living in the Dungeon?" he asked in a surly tone.

"Not that it matters, but I'm staying at the castle right now." I was attempting to be polite.

"Well I think you should take your place where you belong, young lady. You have an image to uphold. Living at the Dungeon is part of it."

He stalked away, disappearing into his cute cottage.

What a grump. It seemed someone hadn't found a fair lady to spend time with him since there was so much upheaval that day.

"Goodnight to you too," I called after him.

I walked over to the Dungeon. The outside door was locked. That was a surprise. It was never locked. Even when Chase and I were in bed, we locked the apartment door, not the outside door. I pounded it in case Canyon was inside. There was no response. I couldn't turn off the noisy prisoners without getting inside.

Not sure who to call about the problem—Chase had keys for every door in the Village—I had forgotten to get them from Canyon. Maybe Bart knew where another set was located. I didn't want to trudge across the wet grass again, but Sam wouldn't be the only one complaining if the tortured prisoners didn't stop moaning.

I pounded on the door again. No answer. If Canyon was inside, he was asleep. I started to head back to Baron's with a few mumbled curses, when I heard another sound from inside that wasn't part of the endless repetition of tortured prisoners.

Was that Canyon? Had he hurt himself?

"Canyon? Are you in there? Did you fall down the stairs? Pound on something if that's you."

I listened again. No pounding. The prisoners kept crying and begging for help. But in that sound, I still heard something that was different than the taped responses. It wasn't anyone calling for help, and there was no pounding.

But what if Canyon couldn't pound on something? What if he was injured? I couldn't just leave him.

There wasn't anything I could use to open the door in a conventional manner. But there was a loose cobblestone that was in this Village and mine. I'd noticed it right away—a pet peeve I frequently complained about. Maintenance never seemed to repair it well enough.

I picked it up and hit the lock on the Dungeon door as hard as I could. I knew it wasn't very solid. It didn't need to be since they wanted people to go in and out. I had to hit it three times before the lock broke and the door opened with a chilling creak that also wasn't part of the soundtrack.

"Hello?"

Chapter Twenty-four

It was dark inside. The light switch was near the stairs to the apartment. I didn't have a flashlight, but I knew this place well. There shouldn't have been a problem walking from the door to the stairs. The prisoners in the jail cells were further inside.

I put my arms out and scuffed my feet, trying to make sure nothing was in the way.

"You shouldn't be here," Starshine whispered. "Go get help. You need help."

"I can reach the light switch without help," I told her. "I'll be fine."

"No, Jessie—"

I lost that argument as I tripped over something on the floor. Maybe nothing should've been there, but it was. Worse, it was lumpy and soft...like a body.

Falling hard over the top of it, I heard a muted cry.

Tension and fear raced up my spine as I crawled the rest of the way to reach the light switch and flipped it on.

Isabelle was tied and gagged on the floor. Her dark hair flowed across her face, but I would have known that green gown anywhere.

"Are you all right?" I untied her and she removed her duct tape gag.

"Do I look all right? Reginald has gone insane. He hit me in the head and grabbed me out of my room. Then he brought me here. Where am I anyway? Why are you here, Jessie?"

I helped her to her feet, immediately thinking about her death in my Village. I shivered at her touch and hoped this wasn't going to be one of those crossover moments. This wasn't how she'd died, but that didn't mean anything.

"You're in the Dungeon. Sir Reginald didn't know to shut off the prisoners." I turned off the soundtrack as I explained. "Why did he bring you here?"

"Because he's insane. Why do you think? Let's get out of here and tell someone."

"I'm the Bailiff," I reminded her. "I'm the one you're supposed to tell."

She laughed. "And you're going to save me from him? Where's Canyon?"

I checked upstairs in the apartment. Canyon wasn't there, and it didn't appear that he had been since he got out of jail, as evidenced by the moldy food on the table. Detective Almond had wanted to see what he would stir up with Canyon's release. Was this it?

"Are you sure it was Sir Reginald?"

"I was standing in my room talking to him. He was flirting with me—like always. I turned back to get a drink, and he cracked me on the head with something. I think I'm bleeding. We need to call a doctor."

She was right. There was blood mixed with her dark hair, and a smear of it on her pale forehead.

"All right. The first thing is to get you to safety. He

doesn't want me, so I'm in no danger."

"He wants me?" She frowned. "What do you mean? He and I have never—would never…"

"I think that was his motivation. He has a thing about his virility and women telling him no. He might be the one who killed the fairy."

"He killed someone? This is making my head hurt. Where do you plan to take me that's safe from him?"

"We have to get out of here," I suggested. "He's changed his MO, moving you somewhere to kill you in secret. He got away with it last time out in the open, but now he's getting sneaky."

"Could you strategize later, and let's hide until the police get here?"

"Yes." I considered where we could go. "There's a big crowd at *Stage Caravan*. We'll go there, and I'll call the police. We should be safe until then."

"Okay. Let's go."

Isabelle was unsteady on her feet. She might be more injured than I'd considered. I put my arm around her so we could move quickly away from the Dungeon. She leaned against me—obviously in bad condition.

I flung open the door to the Dungeon to make our escape, and there was Sir Reginald.

He was wearing armor again. It wasn't the red and black this time but plain dull gray. I didn't think he was afraid of Isabelle hurting him—maybe it was a remembrance of his glory days.

It didn't matter. His long face was as pale as Isabelle's. I could see the disconnect in his eyes. He should've had that heart attack. Maybe it would've stopped this.

"Bailiff," he said calmly. "I see you've found poor Isabelle. The man who killed the fairy and the squire attacked her at the castle. I brought her here to protect her. I had to get her away from him."

"That's a lie unless you're admitting to killing those people," Isabelle accused. "You brought me here because I told you to go away and you were angry."

"She's been injured. Help me get her somewhere safe, Jessie. Then we can call the police."

"I've got her," I said. "You call the police. Let's walk toward the Main Gate so we can meet them there."

I didn't buy his story, but I thought I could throw him off if he believed we were working together. My hand itched to call Detective Almond, but I had to deal with this first. If Sir Reginald had already changed his game plan about strangling people out in the open and advanced to hitting them on the head, he might decide he could kill me too.

"That's a wonderful plan." He stepped to the side of the walkway that led to the cobblestones. "You go first. That way I can help you with her if you need it."

"No! You're crazy," Isabelle squealed. "Stay away from me. Keep him away from me, Jessie. You're the Bailiff. Do something!"

That wasn't helping.

Sir Reginald took out a gun. "Crazy am I, wench? I'll show you!"

"Now would be a good time for some fairy magic," I muttered. "I wish I could get out of this without anyone getting hurt. Starshine?"

She didn't appear, and there was no *poof* of magic that put Sir Reginald in handcuffs and left him waiting for the police. Fair-weather fairies. You just couldn't count on them to do anything useful.

It was up to me. We had to get away from him long enough to call for help.

While he was glaring at Isabelle, I pushed him hard. He fell backward, and the gun went off. Lucky he didn't hit anyone.

"You know it's illegal to have a gun in Renaissance Village," I said.

"Why you—"

"Run!" I said to Isabelle, grabbing her arm.

"Call the police!" She half ran, half stumbled out of the

Dungeon.

We hid against the side of the building, caught between the sounds of the party still going on at *Stage Caravan* and Sir Reginald cursing and banging as he removed his armor.

I turned on the radio, but it wasn't working. *Please charge.* I hit it a few times but nothing.

"What's wrong?" she whispered. "Why isn't it working?"

"It needs to be plugged in." How many times had I heard Chase complain about the radios not having a long enough charge?

"Great! What now?"

"We run."

Not a problem for me, but Isabelle tripped on her pretty gown and fell to the ground after only a few steps.

"I think I twisted my ankle," she moaned.

Of course. Like a bad movie.

"Not now." I urged her to her feet. "He's coming!"

Without his armor, and completely crazy, Sir Reginald was after us like a hound after two foxes. He kept calling Isabelle but didn't shoot anything else. He was probably reserving his bullets for us.

Lucky us.

Isabelle and I couldn't run, but we hobbled away in the darkness. We finally reached the relative safety of *Stage Caravan.* The lights were low, but there were still people talking and playing their mandolins.

"Having someone else here will protect us," I told Isabelle. "And maybe someone has a cell phone."

But as soon as Sir Reginald arrived, he shot three times in the air. What few people were there ran away in a panic. Isabelle and I stood on one side of the the darkened stage, but we would have to pass right in front of the stage lights to get back to the cobblestones. He'd see us for sure.

Behind the stage was only an old privy and some trees.

"He's going to see us," Isabelle whispered. "There's no way around the stage with him standing there."

"We need a diversion." I stared at Sir Reginald. "I'll make some noise over here and when he starts toward me, you go the other way. You'll end up at the blacksmith's shop."

"I can't do that. I can barely walk. I'll make noise, and you get away. Find someone who can call the police."

It was hard for me to imagine that Isabelle could be brave and self-sacrificing. I'd never known her to be that way. She was right, of course. I'd have a better chance of getting away. Except that if I left her, Sir Reginald would probably kill her before I could get back with help.

"That's not going to work, but I have another idea. You go over there and hide in the privy. I don't think he's crazy enough to look in there, do you?"

"My dress will be ruined," she complained. "I'll never get the smell out of it."

"You can get another dress. We're talking about your life, Isabelle. After you get in there, I'll lead Sir Reginald away. You find someone with a phone. Or maybe we'll get lucky and both of us will find someone with a phone. Now get over there. This is as good as it gets."

She still whined and complained about it, but she hobbled to the old privy and stepped inside.

I smiled as I thought of her in the abandoned wooden outhouse. No one knew who'd left it here. The Village used the modern plastic kind that a truck came and emptied every few days. The wooden one covered a hole dug in the ground. We joked about it, but most residents never went near it.

It was a gamble that there was enough of Sir Reginald's arrogance in his addled head that he wouldn't stoop so low to look in there. Then I realized I would have to stay and watch to make sure he didn't find Isabelle. Maybe that was more heroic than I'd ever thought of myself, but I had taken on the office of Bailiff. Chase was strong and brave. I could be too.

"What are you waiting for?" Starshine asked. "Run away. Find someone to call for help."

I peered from behind the back of the stage. "I have to

know if she's safe. Then I can run."

"You're letting this whole thing about being the Bailiff relieve you of your common sense, Jessie. You don't even like Isabelle, and competed for Chase with her. I'm sure you would've been glad to duel with her like Canyon did with Chase."

"This is different. *Shh.* He's coming this way."

The few colored lights from the stage glinted on the large gun he held before him as he walked past me and toward the privy. Starshine stayed where she was at my side. Neither of us moved as he went by.

For just an instant I thought about tackling him and taking the gun away. But even though Sir Reginald was probably in his sixties, he was in fair condition. If I was wrong in even one move, I could be dead, with Isabelle following soon after. I had no doubt that if he shot me, she would scream and run out.

I held my breath as he walked to the privy. I could barely see him glance at it, but I knew the stench was terrible. He covered his face with his free hand and quickly walked away.

Thank you.

He came around the other side of the stage, moving temporary scenery and searching through chairs with his gun ready. He finally gave up a few minutes later and started across the cobblestones toward the King's Highway. There were lights, music, and laughter at Baron's. He was probably going there.

That was fine with me. I knew a dozen merchants who lived upstairs from their shops if I walked toward the castle. That would keep me away from him and get the police here at the same time.

But I hadn't reckoned with Isabelle's low tolerance for stench. She pushed open the cracked wooden door and stumbled out of the privy, coughing and complaining. I ran to shush her, putting my hand over her mouth as I saw Sir Reginald start back toward us.

"This way," I urged her. "We can hide behind the

Dungeon until he passes us again. Quiet."

Chapter Twenty-five

The area in front of the shops and along the cobblestones was mostly kept in good repair with daily use of lawnmowers and trimmers. No one wanted a visitor to stumble or catch their costume in tall grass or weeds.

Behind the shops and rides was a different story. As long as there wasn't any trash back here, the city didn't care how high the grass was, and neither did Adventure Land. This was a no- man's land scattered with cigarette butts and the occasional plastic chair or stump where residents hung out.

This was where Isabelle and I carefully stumbled behind the new privies and the big Tree Swing. Isabelle wouldn't hold her skirt up for fear a snake would bite her, and nothing I could say made any difference. Her ankle was hurt, and she favored it heavily by leaning against me.

Of course this would be a night when no one was outside smoking, singing, or fooling around in the dark where they wouldn't be seen. We had to keep going until we reached the back of the Dungeon where we paused to rest for a moment.

"I can't go on," Isabelle said dramatically. "I'm in so much pain. I need someone to carry me."

I couldn't see her face in the darkness to know if she was joking.

"I'm not carrying you. I'm not Chase or Canyon. You're going to have to limp along until we find someone or I'll have to leave you here."

"You wouldn't leave me, Jessie. You didn't leave me back there. I think you have the same outdated ideas about loyalty and bravery like Chase does. I guess you two really belong together."

"Now isn't a good time to test that theory," I murmured, listening for Sir Reginald. I knew she was trying to get what she wanted by any means necessary. It was what she'd always done with Chase.

"I don't know what else to do." She sobbed. "I can only stand so much agony."

By this time, I was certain that someone from *Stage Caravan* would've alerted the police. Or someone at the castle would have heard shots fired in the Village. Where were the police sirens? Someone should have been here by now. I shouldn't have to drag Isabelle all the way to the castle.

She was moaning. Short of putting a gag in her mouth, I didn't know what to do. Isabelle was small but not small enough for me to carry.

"Come on," I said. "You've rested long enough. The *Jolly Pipe Maker shop* is next. If we're lucky, maybe someone will be out there playing checkers.'

"Who?"

"Never mind. Let's go." I helped her to her feet. I could barely walk because she was leaning so heavily against me. "You have to shift some of your weight, Isabelle. We aren't going to get anywhere like this."

"Are you saying I'm fat?"

"No. I'm saying I'm not a pack mule. You have to move your feet too."

"You've never liked me, Jessie." She started crying again. "It was always more than just about Chase. You hate me, don't you?"

"Of course I don't hate you. I just want to get out of here before Sir Reginald finds us."

"I always wondered why you wanted to take Chase from me. Now I know."

"Shut up and walk, Isabelle. It's not time for you to die yet—at least I don't think it is."

Her face was very close to mine. "Are you saying you wish I was dead even though I agreed to give up Chase for you?"

"I don't wish you were dead. But you had nothing to do with me and Chase getting together. Please try to walk. Sir Reginald could be on us if we don't get out of here."

She sat down hard in the grass along the side of the cobblestones and refused to move. "I'm tired. My feet hurt. I probably have a concussion, and I smell like privy. I'm not moving until someone comes for me."

"Not a problem, my dear." Sir Reginald was right behind us. He shoved the gun in my face. "Jessie, you and I have unfinished business once I take care of this little slut."

"Slut?" Isabelle started crying again. "Why are people always saying mean things about me?"

He raised the gun toward her head. "Goodbye, my lady."

I probably should have reacted. Thrown myself between the gun and Isabelle, but I was too tired and disgusted with her to care.

She screamed but there was no gunshot. The lights were dim but not dim enough that I couldn't see Sir Reginald trying to fire the gun over and over. The click of the trigger brought no response. He was out of bullets.

Sighing at my fate, I threw myself against him. He managed to hit me a few times in the arm with his gun before I got it away from him. He was strong, but I had him at a disadvantage since I was on top of him, beating him with my fists and kicking him.

I heard Isabelle get to her feet. I was foolish enough to think she was going to jump on him too. Instead she vanished into the darkness, screaming for help. Maybe that would bring someone from one of the parties into our direction. Maybe not. I held on to Sir Reginald and kept pummeling him until he was lying still beneath me.

Exhausted, I rolled off him and on the grass. I could barely catch my breath. I heard people running in our direction. The stadium lights from the Village Green came on. Suddenly I could see everything.

Sir Reginald was gasping for breath too. His face was white and drawn. A police car came through the Main Gate with lights and sirens blaring. A few residents stood away from me and Sir Reginald watching to see what would happen next.

Knowing what I did about the other Sir Reginald, I immediately started CPR on him. It was weird putting my mouth on his after punching him there a few minutes earlier. I pushed hard on his chest to make him breathe and finally someone pulled me aside and took my place.

"Are you okay, Jessie?" Chase asked.

I looked at Canyon. He was on the ground with Sir Reginald. "I think he had a heart attack."

"We saw Isabelle. She told us what happened. A few people from *Stage Caravan* had come over to Baron's talking about a fight. We just didn't know they were talking about you."

Chase put his arms around me, and I leaned against him. I don't know how Bailiff-like it was, and I didn't care. The ambulance finally arrived and had to push Isabelle aside to make room for Sir Reginald, promising they would send another vehicle back for her.

Sir Reginald might recover from his heart attack here. One of the paramedics said that some people went out of their heads when they were having problems with their heart—something about not getting enough oxygen to the brain. Maybe the crusty, old knight would still make it to fulfill his job as manager of the castle.

"Are you sure you don't need to go to the hospital?" Chase asked as we started walking toward the castle. All the outside lights were on now making the Village much brighter. Dozens of residents had come out to see what was going on.

"I'm fine. Just a little sore. Nothing a hot shower won't help."

"I think we can take care of that, and I do a pretty good back rub too." He smiled down at me. "You know, all of this has started me thinking about what you said."

"That you should be the next Bailiff?"

"Yes. I was glad I could be there when the horse crashed into the bleachers. I wish I could've been here to protect you and Isabelle. I think I could be good at it."

"I think you're right. We'll have to have some kind of duel or something to see who gets to be Bailiff."

He stopped walking. "Canyon said he's not interested anymore."

"I'm still Bailiff. I was talking about me." I stared at him without smiling. "I think I'm good at this."

"Come on. You don't want to duel." He wrapped his arms around me again. "It was your idea for me to be the next Bailiff."

"We'll see. I may be willing to take you on as an apprentice until you learn the ropes. Don't forget you have to live in the Dungeon if you're the Bailiff."

He picked me up and put me over his shoulder. I screamed and laughed all the way back to the castle. It didn't take long to run a hot bath instead of a shower. We shared it and then shared a bottle of wine before we went to bed.

I was almost asleep when I heard Starshine tell me goodnight. I was too tired to reply and fell asleep with my head against Chase's shoulder. There was always tomorrow to talk to her about what I needed to do next.

* * *

"Time to wake up, sleepy head." Chase playfully slapped my butt under the blanket.

"After last night, I think I get to sleep in today. Someone else will have to be Bailiff. Maybe you could start training yourself."

"What are you talking about? I know you don't like the fairy convention, but you can't have my job to get away from it. That wouldn't help anyway. I probably see more fairies every ten minutes than you do all day at the museum."

Museum?

I lifted my head and glanced around the room with one eye open.

This was it. I was home at my Dungeon.

There was a custom-made wedding band on my hand that matched Chase's. I'd finally done it. I was back in my Village.

"You aren't going to believe where I've been." I sat up to tell him. "You probably didn't even miss me with the dead fairy investigation going on."

"Oh yeah. We figured that out last night. I didn't want to wake you. I'm afraid the new guy, the one you hired to help me, was the one who killed the fairy."

"Canyon?" That really caught my attention. "What do you mean? It wasn't Lord Dunstable or Sir Reginald?"

"No. You must've dreamed that. Canyon admitted that he killed her. He said he has a problem with women who reject him. Her friend actually witnessed the whole thing but was afraid to tell us. I talked to her again, and she spilled everything. Canyon folded when I found him."

I followed Chase to the kitchen—our kitchen—and stared at him as he made pancakes.

"I can't believe Canyon killed her. He had excellent references."

"Besides his record for assaults against women?"

"What? I checked his police records. There were no assaults."

He hugged me. "You did the best you could."

Then it occurred to me. "We can still go on our honeymoon?"

"Sure." He kissed me. "I think I need a vacation. I'm finally finished with that mess my father and Morgan made too. Let's do something fun."

I hugged him and squealed. "Awesome. When do we leave?"

"Not until the fairies are gone at the end of the week," he said. "They need you here for the museum, and I have to be here because my new assistant is in jail."

"Sorry."

He handed me a plate of pancakes. "Next time, let me hire my own assistant."

"But you won't," I argued. "You need help, Chase. You can't do this by yourself."

"You're right. As soon as we come back from vacation, I'll hire an assistant who can get up at three a.m. and tell the security guards what to do. Okay?"

"Yes." I smeared my pancakes with maple syrup, happy to be home again. Only one thing bothered me. "You didn't even realize I was gone, did you?"

He sat across from me with his pancakes and raised his brows. "Gone? You mean you left the museum early yesterday? Yeah. Manny told me."

"No. I was gone like I left the Village."

"Where did you go?"

I started thinking before I told him I'd gone to another Village where he and I weren't together. It hadn't happened. It looked as though I'd dreamed the whole thing.

"I went to the store." I shrugged. "I was only gone a little while. It was nothing."

We finished breakfast together, and Chase had to go. He'd already received calls for various problems in the short time we'd been eating.

I showered and put on my tan gown with the large pockets. The fairies weren't going to get me down with their skimpy outfits. Chase and I were together. Life was good. I would never make a stupid wish again.

When I hit the cobblestones headed toward the *Art and Craft Museum*, the Village was teaming with fairies. I'd never seen so many. There were tall fairies, short fairies, blue and green fairies. Most of them had wings although a few just wore capes.

I smiled into the sunshine as I approached the museum. Mrs. Potts from the *Honey and Herb Shoppe* waved to me. I wasn't looking where I was going as I waved back and stumbled against someone.

"Oh! Excuse me," a very familiar voice said.

I looked down, and there was Starshine. She was wearing the same hooded blue cloak and gown with ruffles at the bottom. But she was walking along the cobblestones, barely three feet tall.

"It's you!" I grinned and moved out of her way. "I wasn't sure if I'd see you again."

"I wasn't sure if you saw me at all since you almost stepped on me."

"I'm sorry. I'm used to you being up higher." I held my hand at my waist. "You know—with your wings buzzing—while you're flying."

"Buzzing wings? Flying?" She frowned and turned her back to me. "You must be thinking of someone else, young woman. I don't wear wings. I like my hood and cloak."

"Oh. I understand." I whispered, "You're worried about people knowing who you are. I get it."

"Yes." She cleared her throat. "Well, it's very nice to meet you." She held out her tiny hand. "I hope we'll see each other again under better circumstances."

Was I wrong? Had I imagined having a fairy godmother too? I felt stupid as I shook her hand. "I hope you have a wonderful time in Renaissance Village. Please come and visit me at the *Art and Craft Museum*."

"*Huzzah!*" She giggled.

I left it at that. When you're not sure what's real, the best thing is to know that you don't know.

"Goodbye, Jessie."

I looked back, and she was moving away from me with a quick smile and a wink.

"Goodbye, Fairy Godmother. And thank you for everything."

About the Authors

Joyce and Jim Lavene write award-winning, bestselling mystery and urban fantasy fiction as themselves, J.J. Cook, and Ellie Grant. Their first mystery novel, Last Dance, won the Master's Choice Award for best first mystery novel in 1999. Their romance, Flowers in the Night, was nominated for the Frankfurt Book Award in 2000.

They have written and published more than 70 novels for Harlequin, Penguin, Amazon, and Simon and Schuster that are sold worldwide. They have also published hundreds of non-fiction articles for national and regional publications. They live in Midland, North Carolina with their family and their rescue pets—Rudi, Stan Lee, and Quincy.

Visit them at:
www.joyceandjimlavene.com
www.facebook.com/joyceandjimlavene
http://amazon.com/author/jlavene
https://twitter.com/AuthorJLavene

Other books in this series

Book 1 – Wicked Weaves – ISBN **9780425223307**
Book 2 – Ghastly Glass – ISBN **9780425230305**
Book 3 – Deadly Daggers – ISBN **9780425236444**
Book 4 – Harrowing Hats – ISBN **9780425242773**
Book 5 – Treacherous Toys – ISBN **9780425251584**
Book 5.5 – Perilous Pranks – a novella
ASIN: **B00EJMVTDM** – Only for Kindle
Book 6 – Murderous Matrimony –
ISBN: **9781494874919** – ASIN: **B00GOA74N6**
Book 7 – Bewitching Boots –
ISBN: **978-1500683412** – ASIN: **B00M9NZN4E**

CPSIA information can be obtained
at www.ICGtesting.com
Printed in the USA
LVHW051536120121
676309LV00013B/1340